Worldship Files – V

By Erik Schubach

Self publishing

P.O. Box 523

Nine Mile Falls, WA 99026

This is a work of fiction. Any resemblance to real persons, living or dead, is purely coincidental.

Manufactured in the United States of America

FIRST EDITION

ISBN 9798674538967

CHAPTER 1
Land Grab

We followed behind the Fae delegation from the Delta Stack's A-Ring as we made our way to yet another meeting with the newly elected mayor of the Cityship, Redemption. I was assigned as a guide for the mayor, an elderly human female named Tamera Lynn Abara, who had lost the sight in one eye due to the radiation damage she took in her long life aboard the failing Cityship and its twin, the Yammato.

The new magi-tech cybernetic replacement was an uncanny match to her piercing brown eye that told the story of a hard life that she had weathered and survived. In the six months since our first contact with the Cityships as they approached our Worldship, Leviathan, the majority of the people on the failing Cityships sought treatment for various maladies that would have been cured easily with our magic assisted medical technology. We were on our ten thousand year journey to our new home on the planet Eridani Prime.

In these intervening months, the Leviathan has been undergoing extensive repairs herself, from the ill-fated attack by the fanatical group called the Outliers, who had taken the Cityships by force long ago, in the belief that what we had on the Leviathan was destined to be theirs.

They, and their leader, Richter, found that destiny had other plans as they paid with their lives. But we paid a steep price to defend against their cowardly human purist sneak attack. Both in personnel and damage to the ring stacks, when their people went after the Fae in the upper rings of the mammoth rotating ring stacks which made up our world.

All the hull damage has been repaired, the skin jockeys working double shifts for months to ensure we were space-worthy again. Now efforts have switched to repairing the internal damage wrought. The delicate environmental balances in the rings will take years to recover, even with the help of the magic from the various magical races that we humans shared the world with.

That was ultimately the downfall of the Outliers, the Human purists who believed the magical races took what was rightfully theirs and that humans toiled as their servants. None of them had ever seen, or met, any of the preternatural races before, and had certainly only heard about magic in the stories of old Earth since all the magical races left Earth over five thousand years ago aboard the Leviathan.

When the Outliers came up against real magic, they found that they were not just ill-prepared for it, but that they were completely helpless against it.

They had no idea that while it was true that to some extent, Humans are looked down upon by many of the races, we are all equal in the eyes of the law and share this amazing world. Well, for the most part, since the Fae stick almost exclusively to the upper A and B Rings, and only follow the laws of the world as a courtesy.

It is because of the magic Fae artifacts stored in the Ka'Ifinitum that the massive world drives and other systems on the ship work, as they would require more power than the multiple cold fusion and quantum decay powerplants can provide. It is this fusion of magic and technology... magi-tech, that our world is possible. So they sort of had a bargaining chip that gives them special dispensation in just about any matter, since they can just stop providing power to just about any system in the lower rings if they are displeased.

Even with that, the world worked, and the stacks spun, and we all lived in relative harmony. Yes, that was a qualifier, relative, since there are always those who break the laws in any society, and the Leviathan is no different. So the Brigade Enforcers like me, Knith Shade, are there as the law enforcers for the world.

Now that we're getting back to a semblance of normalcy in the aftermath of the attack, enterprising individuals and corporations have been finding ways to leverage the addition of the two ailing Cityships to our community, now that the people of the Cityships have voted nearly unanimously to become part of our shared journey under the governance of the Leviathan's elected body.

The critical repairs to their systems are now completed, and new radiation shielding put in place, and their hydroponics and agricultural domes being replenished by our teams and the nature elementals and other magical beings.

Their life support, bolstered by our more efficient systems, can now support almost twice their meager complement of twenty-five thousand people per ship. This has created almost a gold rush, as my girlfriend, Princess Aurora of the Winter Court of the Fae tells me, “One thing there is never any more of, is land, but now, there is so much open space unused in the Cityships, it is creating a land grab.”

I get the general idea, but some of the terms are foreign to me. Being merely human, born on the Leviathan almost five thousand years into her journey, and never seeing Open Air, or old Earth before, as she had in her youth, I didn't get a lot of the archaic references my girl uttered. Since Fae are essentially eternal, it seems like a short time ago for her, when it was generations ago for people like me.

And since I'm in charge of the Fae and Brigade Liaison Enforcers, I cringe at the FABLE acronym; I have had to accompany all the representatives from the Cityships when they meet with any Fae on the world, to act as a buffer.

Since the people from the Redemption and Yammato are not familiar with the dangers of dealing with the Fae, lucky me gets to play chaperon. Just simple mistakes like saying thank you to a Fae could wind up with you being beholden to them for life and beyond if you aren't careful. And these city-dwellers are naive to the trickery of the Fae and almost blindly walk into deals that only benefit the Fae.

Even the Summer Fae, the Seelie, who are supposed to be the gentler side of the Fae are tricksters. And even though no greater Fae can lie, they can deceive even more ruthlessly by twisting the truth.

I cringed when the Mayor of the Yammato blindly agreed to lease land in one of the agri-domes for a Fae vineyard. Pledging workers to help maintain the grapevines and water from their processing plants. But if they would have taken a moment to actually assess what they were offering in return for some meager salaries for the workers, they were taking a loss in the agreement, the cost of water processing and supply would far outweigh the employment of a few workers. But Fae contracts are binding once signed, even if they take advantage of the poor soul who walks into them without both eyes open.

Ignorance of the Fae is no defense in contract law, I should know. I absently raised a hand to my lips, one burning with Summer's living fire, and the other the crystal blue ice of Winter. Yup, I was the only person in history to have ever been boneheaded and unlucky enough to be cursed by both of the Queens of the Seelie and Unseelie courts.

The buzz of wings next to my ear from my Sprite companion, Graz, and she muttered, “Bonehead.” She always knew when I was lamenting my own bad luck. I flicked her wings and she giggled at me.

"Jerk. Shut up and let me work here. And what are you even doing here, this is Brigade business," I whispered.

Mayor Abara prompted, turning her age creased face toward me, dark freckling showing on her ebony skin, which gave her so much character, "What was that, dear?"

I smiled down at the short woman, who was walking taller now that crippling arthritis that had almost doubled her over to look even shorter when I first met her had healed. "Nothing, ma'am. Was just dealing with an annoying buzz in my ear."

Her smile bloomed as her eyes went from me to Graz, who just made a so there grunt in my ear and buzzed over to sit on the woman's shoulder. The Mayor was pleased as a Faun in zero-g as she looked at the flying pain in my ass with adoration. Graz stuck her tongue out at me as the woman cooed at her. "So pretty and such delicate wings. And you can talk?"

Graz patted her shoulder. "Yes I can, granny Big. You're the Will-o'-the wisp's light yerself."

Great, she was making friends, the poor woman wouldn't be able to get rid of her if she kept encouraging the little flying pest, but I found I was smiling despite myself. As annoying as Graz can be, she was pretty much my best friend, and she had a way... an abrasive way, of making people a little less anxious.

So I may have grown a little fond of her and her family basically taking over my nightstand without my permission and making it their home. The kids were adorable, even if the kleptomaniac pollinator of their family was such a pain at times.

I told the Mayor as we walked, “Fae are tricky and won't offer anything that doesn't benefit themselves more than you. They can twist the truth to make it seem they are being sincere, so really digest each and every word and every meaning before you sign anything. And never thank a Greater Fae. They will see it as you acknowledging a debt to them and they will collect.”

She furrowed her brow. “But in the briefing, we were told the Fae could not lie because of some sort of curse or something.”

I smiled as I shook my head. “They can't, but they...”

A smooth, rich voice next to me said, “...are tricksters, and...”

The mayor let out a startled gasp, but I was spinning, one hand drawing an MMG as my other hand grabbed the hand that was reaching for my shoulder while the helmet visor of my Scatter Armor flicked shut. The Fae Lord froze with the barrel of the Magic Mitigating Gun in his face, but his arm never even budged with my hand grasping it. It wasn't that I was holding his arm still, it was that the Greater Fae are just that much stronger than Humans that I couldn't move it.

A huff like a snort behind me had the Leviathan's AI, Mother, displaying a three hundred and sixty-degree view in my heads up display from my helmet cams and an overall view of the corridor from one of her surveillance cameras that were just about everywhere on the world.

I told the Minotaur that had a stun gun pressed against the back of my neck, “You might want to lower the weapon, big guy. Look to your right.”

The huge man turned, his horns sweeping and he froze as he came eyeball to the needle-sharp blade. Graz growled at him, “What, are you stupid ya big cow? She's Brigade, look at the damn armor. I'd do as she says, or I'm havin' eyeball souffle with the family tonight.”

The Fae Lord patted the air with the hand of the arm I still grasped. “It's ok Karthus. I assume that young Miss Shade here is no threat. Besides, from the waves I've watched, I doubt you could take her. Oh don't pout, I'm sorry but it's true.”

The huge man huffed again and holstered his illegal weapon and took a step back from me and Graz's blade. Then the Fae Lord looked at me sheepishly, his face a work of art like all Greater Fae was expressive as he said, “They said there would be Brigade security assigned to the Mayor. I had assumed a couple junior officers. Aren't you a little overkill... Shade.”

He said my name with amusement like he thought I didn't know the name the Fae nurses at the Reproduction Clinic where I was born to maintain Equilibrium of the Human population was an inside joke. In Old Fae, Shade means nobody. And that's who I was when I was born. Just another number to keep the population stable, not born to any family, not having any parents. Us CCs or Clinic

Children were sort of looked down upon as disposable because of the stigma attached to our existence.

I looked at the pretty boy and he said, “I'm Lord Lauran of the Summer Court, son of Queen Titania. I am heading the negotiations with the Cityship Redemption's representative. We didn't mean to startle you.”

I released him and holstered my MMG, and belying his self assured confidence he was exuding, he did take a step back, distancing himself from me. Sometimes I hated the reputation I had been building, but at other times, I enjoyed it, like now. “It's a bad idea to step up to and reach out for a Brigade officer without announcing yourself.” Then I added with eyes narrowed, parrying the humor he enjoyed at my name, “That's how you can lose a hand.”

Ah, there it was, the flash of anger in his eyes at that since I had taken his youngest brother's hand when he had tried to kill me. I know, it was a petty thing to do, but I'm not a complete goody-two-shoes. He recovered in an instant and then made a gracious sweeping gesture with his arm to us and followed us into a crowded conference room. “Yes. I do apologize for that as it was not our intent to catch you off guard.”

He was good, I'd give him that. Then he slapped at the air when the much more nimble Graz buzzed around his head, pointing two fingers at her eyes then his before flying into my helmet to land on my shoulder, grasping my earlobe as we walked.

I turned to Karthus, gesturing to his stunner. “You have a license for that thing?”

Lauran assured me before the Minotaur could respond. “He has all the proper licenses, he's a registered bodyguard for the Seelie.”

I cocked a brow, realizing just how far down the food chain this guy was, since the most important of the children of the Queens of either court, had palace guards who accompanied them everywhere. But then again, this was the Delta stack. So even though it was an A-Ring, it was basically the Greater Fae the Queens preferred to keep at a distance from the palaces.

Then he added, “One can't be too careful, as we all know what happened the last time we greeted the Cityships with open arms.”

Mayor Abara, paused in her fascinated perusal of the overly muscular Minotaur, likely he was the first one she had ever seen. A flash of her own anger lit her eyes a moment but she stayed composed.

I didn't point out that the guard was just for show since we knew that he was the dangerous one, with greater strength than his bodyguard, not to mention the high-level magic the Greater Fae possessed. Karthus was for show. But I did point out since the Redemption official was too composed. “That wasn't the people of the Cityships, it was the Outliers. These people were held by those fanatics.” He knew this too.

I told her, “He's trying to start the negotiations in a position of power.”

She nodded and said, “Young man, I was negotiating deals long before you were even born. Please, let's not play games.”

Ok, that was funny and I had to put my hand over my mouth to hide the smile. Again, she was forgetting that the Fae were not the young adults they all seemed. Lord Lauran was likely thousands of years old. But I'd still wager that she had more life experience. Being short-lived people, Humans had a lot of living to do in our brief two-century lifespans. And from what I heard, the people of the Cityships were lucky to live seventy or eighty years. Mother Fairy humper, I'd be over halfway through my life then if I was born there.

I whispered in her ear, “All of Titania's children were born before the Exodus of the Worldship from Earth.”

Her eyes closed as if she were chastising herself for not remembering her orientation on the Fae and the other preternatural beings on the world.

She inclined her head in apology to the amused looking Fae, who was likely seeing an easy mark. Then he looked up at me as he held the chair for the Mayor to sit at one end of the conference room table. Then as he walked past me, he stopped and said without looking, “I don't remember it being the job of a Brigade Enforcer to coach dignitaries in their negotiations.”

I murmured low so only his Fae ears could pick up, “And I don't remember any of the other negotiations not being held in Verd'real

Palace or even the minor Summer retreat of Verd'secundun in the Gamma Stack."

The man stepped past me, then chuckled as he took his place at the far end of the table as his chuckle became a full laugh. All eyes in the room were on him. A couple other Fae who were obviously his subordinates laughed nervously with him, their brows furrowed in confusion. The man pointed at me as I took my place at the door, opposite his own bodyguard. "I see now why mother is so frustrated with you, Knith Shade. I think I may like you."

Oh hells, I smirked at the man. He wasn't actually too bad... for a Fae. Mother, eavesdropping on my surface thoughts in my helmet, said into my head, "But your mate is Fae, Knith."

I thought loudly to her. "Stop eavesdropping on my thoughts."

"Then stop thinking them so loudly."

Ok, I had no comeback for that, so I internally pouted at her and informed her primly, "Aurora, is my favorite Fae."

Mother made a pleased sound. I wondered absently if she knew just how alive she was when she did things like that that her AI network definitely wasn't programmed to do. She was self-aware, and desperately hiding that fact from the Fae. But she trusted me and Graz with her secret, and I loved her for it.

"What's not to love?" she squeaked out.

"What did I just say about listening to... you know what, never mind. This is going to be a long day of just standing here, could you..."

“On it, Knith.” And a song from the archaeological music archives started blaring in my head as I watched the meeting begin as all the introductions were made. I had to physically restrain my foot from tapping to a band humorously called Five Finger Death Punch was playing a tune called “Wrong Side of Heaven” as the immensely boring negotiations for some of the heavily damaged habitat ring of the Cityship for a vacation resort began.

When had my life been relegated to this? What I wouldn't do for some excitement or even adventure right about now?

CHAPTER 2

Sword of Damocles

I have to admit that the negotiation was a little more interesting than I thought it might be. I mean, the Fae are used to people fawning over them. Men and women of most of the races idealized them and acted like groupies at an Irontown Clank concert in the Beta-C ring.

They haven't dealt with a woman wizened with age, who could appreciate the pretty wrapper, but not be charmed by the person beneath it. I realized that she'd do well in the negotiation for the most part when she interrupted Lord Lauran almost immediately when he tried to lead the negotiations by starting out, declaring for the record that the negotiations were between his holdings in the Summer Court and the Cityship Redemption.

She spoke over him, "Point of order, young man. The Cityship Sojourner. When the Outliers mutinied and took over the ship and the Yammato, before destroying the other Cityships of non-believers, they renamed the Sojourner to Redemption, to reflect their warped vision of wresting the Leviathan and the Ka'Ifinitum from the hands of the magical races that they had deemed cockroaches."

Then she inclined her head. "So the reclaiming of our original name was ratified just this morning with the city council of our vessel."

Lauran's eyes looked frustrated that she had interrupted his flow, but his smooth and likely practiced smile didn't reflect it. "Of course Madame Mayor. Negotiations between the Summerland holdings of Lord Lauran, and the Cityship Sojourner."

She smiled as if to give praise to a misguided child, and I knew at that moment that she was one of my favorite humans ever. I know it sounds like I don't have any great love for the Fae, I am after all, hopelessly in love with the slightly rebellious Princess Aurora of the Winter Court. It's just that seeing the people who have come out on the losing end of Greater Fae contracts, and having been taken by a Fae Lord who cut me open to harvest my eggs, and then attempted to kill me afterward, makes me a little reticent to embrace them as a whole.

Add to that, the fact the Fae Queens have each seen fit to place their mark on me without my consent, and you can see where I may not be the best person to cheer them on. I know there are good Fae and bad Fae, but some stuff is hard to get over. I'm overly fond of quite a few in the Winter and one or two in the Summer courts as well, so there is that.

I may or may not have prompted Mayor Abara on a few points where it came to the infrastructure the city would pledge to the resort Lauran was wanting to build. Just a shake of a head here, a nod there, causing the man to keep looking back at me at the door, sure I was doing what he suspected.

He had huffed in exasperation when they were about to sign the contract but, I was miming drinking from an invisible glass, warning in my eyes, which got her to hesitate and read the wording on the resources the city would provide the resort. She tapped it with a finger as she said, “We hadn't discussed where the water was coming from to fill the artificial lagoon and waterfall, the centerpiece of your resort, dear boy.”

He smiled at her in accommodation as he said between clenched teeth as he looked back at me, “Of course we did, Madame Mayor. Where it is mentioned on page two hundred and thirty-three of the agreement, which states the Cityship will supply the basic utilities to run the resort in exchange for employing fifty residents in the grounds-keeping and systems maintenance departments.”

She smirked. “I'm sure it was just an oversight by the Fae, to equate the most valuable substance in existence, water, as a basic utility. Where we agree to supply that necessity to the dwelling units of the resort, supplying the thousands of tons of water for your water feature, a non-necessity, would tax our water extraction and reclamation systems and cause shortages in our hydroponics and agri-domes.”

The woman was crossing things out and handwriting things in as she spoke. Then she looked up with the sweetest smile. Not being able to lie, he just stated, “I'll have to speak with our legal team about how that got in there.” Spinning the truth, since all he had to do to make it true was to ask, even if he knew it was himself that had included the broadly vague statement in the contract.

She just looked at him expectantly until he inclined his head. "Of course the Summer Court would pay to install another ore processor to extract water from the crushed regolith mined from the asteroid attached to the Yammato."

The woman added, "And the transport of the ore to the Sojourner... of course"

The man actually smiled in genuine mirth, which reached his twinkling eyes as he bowed slightly in his chair. "You, lady, would make a spectacular Fae. We agree with your stipulation." The other Fae in the room gasped or groaned at him.

She beamed a smile back as she hastily scribbled in the contract as he stood and walked around the table, stopping at her side, then shooting me a smarmy grin as he initialed her changes, then they both signed the document. He and the other Greater Fae stabbed their fingers with their Ionga rings on their thumbs and smeared blood on the signatures, and magic flared, sealing the deal with that magic.

That was the first time I witnessed a contract sealed that way and I blinked in surprise as I learned something. I had always wondered what the Ionga rings stood for, but apparently, they were to extract blood from the pinprick the sharp point could administer since Greater Fae would heal the wound instantly.

Mother told me, “All you had to do was ask. I swear, I often wonder if Graz is right about you at times, but I prefer to believe your intelligence is underestimated.”

“Stop sifting through my head.”

“Then stop yelling.” And she had to add, “Rory is right, you are cute when you're flustered.”

“I hate you both.”

“No, you don't.”

“No,, I don't, I love you, but don't push it, lady.”

I smiled when she chuckled, then froze when Lauran, who was watching me as the contract was bound by magic, smiled bigger. Just space me now, he thought I was smiling at him.

Graz had my back. “What's wrong with you, ya stupid Big, you look like you're stroking out or something.”

The man's smile was replaced with annoyance, and I felt and tasted magic building, small sparks were drizzling from his fingertips. He was going to bug-zap Graz, the thin-skinned jerk. I lifted a hand. “I wouldn't do...”

Too late, he flicked his finger, and a small spark of magic hurled toward the buzzing Sprite.

I closed my eyes and shook my head. Why me? I heard the man's startled yelp first, knowing Graz had avoided his casting and was likely showering the man with hexed dust to cause his skin to break out in hives as she squeaked, “Don't go slinging your cut-rate

Summer magics at me, you oversize Fairy turd. I'll kick your flower-loving a..."

I droned out in resignation, "Graz, stop."

"Alright, but you saw it, he attacked. That's an act of war against Winter and..."

"And nothing. That was him being annoyed with you. And he didn't even hit you with it."

"Damn straight. The day a Big like him gets the drop on me..."

"Like when Richter caught you in a jar?"

"Ooooo low. Fine."

She crossed her arms across her chest and buzzed backward to land on the Mayor's shoulder while she glared at Lauran, who was looking highly uncomfortable as he adjusted his collar while red welts started appearing on all his exposed skin.

I looked around the room at everyone staring at the dust-up as if in incomprehension and said as I stepped forward to offer an arm to the Mayor, "And with that, if the negotiation is over, I can escort you back to your quarters in the A-Ring of Beta Stack."

It had surprised the heck out of me when Queen Mab of all people had offered a cottage near a stream by a lake in the A-Ring to the visiting Mayor since she had three days of negotiations with various groups on the World before she was ferried back to her city which orbited the Leviathan a hundred miles out.

But the two got along surprisingly well. And Aurora explained to me that Mab, for all her bluster and scary as hell power, had always had a soft spot in her heart for the Human servants she had on old Earth so long ago. And was always saddened when they reached the end of their brief lives. She called them her Fireflies. Whenever I heard things like that, it was always a shock to hear that the scariest woman I knew, had a heart. But I've witnessed it when she visits her Firewyrm or speaks of Aurora when she isn't frustrated with her.

We led her out to the sleek waiting Fae vehicle which looked like a hovering white stingray, then Graz hopped into my helmet as I mounted my Tac-Bike and put on the strobing lights and led the autonomous vehicle back to my home Stack.

On the way down into the Trunk, so we could traverse to the Beta spokes, Mother spoke out loud in my helmet, “This can't be good. The priority channels started lighting up a few minutes ago. Your name is coming up.”

“What's going on?”

“You know I can't tell you that Knith, it's the priority channel.”

“Pleeeease?”

“I don't know why I let you talk me into things like this. But just expect to be called away any minute now. That's all I'm saying. And the Queens. Nothing else. And Princess Aurora.”

I chuckled at the blabbermouth, glad she was on my side.

“Always, Knith.”

I sent a mental hug.

Gaz moaned, “I shoulda went with granny Big. You two sound like an old married couple. I should know since I married a couple.”

I snorted despite myself, but I had to admit that was a pretty funny play on a mated trio of a trinary sex race.

Then Mother wondered aloud, something she was more and more prone to do around us, not having to hide that she was self-aware, “Can AI's ever marry? Or is it just for organics?”

We just completed the trunk transit and were heading up-ring in a Beta Stack spoke, when I was about to retort about being organic, but she interrupted, “The call is coming in now.”

She answered the line for me before I could, and in my voice, she said, “Enforcer Knith Shade.”

I whispered a reprimand, “Mother!”

Rory asked, “What was that Knith? Is there interference on this line?”

“No, just some annoying pests over here. To what do I owe the honor of the most ravishing...”

“Knith, love, please don't try to flirt. You're not very good at it, and you've already won my heart.”

I felt my cheeks burning as I smiled... right up until Graz made little kissy noises next to my ear. And of course, my Fae girlfriend overheard and said in a cheerfully delighted tone, “Hello Graz. Is she staying out of trouble?”

What?!

The traitorous Sprite just responded, her crush on my girl evident as she almost sang back, “Hello your highness. Just fielding a lover's spat between Knith and her work wife.”

I slapped my helmet, causing her to tumble down into my armor. As she squirmed and buzzed her wings to scramble her way back into my helmet, Aurora said with what sounded like a smile in her tone, “Hello Mother.”

I blurted, “She's not my work wife!” A pause then, “Wait... what's a work wife?”

Mother stated in a tin can computerized tone with no emotion, “Hello Princess Aurora of House Ashryver.”

My girl growled in frustration. “Come now, Mother. Aren't we past this yet? I've heard you emoting with Knith and Graz on multiple occasions. You should know by now that your secret is safe with me.”

“Please rephrase your query.”

“Oh fine, play your games.” Then to me, she said, “A meeting has been called in the presidential hall on Beta-B. The lead engineers have completed their sustainability report for our new space caravan, and it mustn't be good news as the President, the cabinet, and the Queens and their most tech-savvy advisors are requested to be present. I'll need a proper escort as I'm giving my royal guard the day off.”

I heard the complaints from her side and I smiled as she didn't bother muting the line as she shushed her guards. “Oh come now.

Do you truly believe I am safer with you, or the Enforcer who tilts at spacecraft?"

I groaned at that, would I never live it down? Did people know how monumentally stupid I had been? And it wasn't bravery or skill that I had come out less of a wreck than the enemy? It was pure dumb luck. Well, that and I had a literal god at my back when Mac outed himself as Oberon, slinging lightning in space. Why hadn't he gotten even half the news waves? I mean, hello, King of the Fae returned from the dead? Anyone?

To my amusement though, they gave up their fight as she said, "I thought not, Now shoo, take the day off, don't make a liar out of me."

I could imagine her guards deflating and trudging out the door then past Nyx, secretary and personal assistant to Princess Aurora. And how the only awkward Fae I knew would stand up as straight as a board, an old fashioned notepad and pen in hand, ready to take a note for the Princess when the doors swung open. The poor girl. One day, I'm sure Rory will actually need a note taken, and Nyx would be her girl.

Mother cleared her throat in my mind. I cocked an eyebrow, then prompted my wayward royal, "Half-truth? Why am I really going?"

She almost giggled, and her laughter sounded like the chiming of silver leaves in an impossible, glittering grove. "The truth is that I require a proper escort to this meeting. Just because mother and

Titania both requested your presence at the meeting is a happy coincidence."

"Why did they..."

"As usual, I believe the Queens already know why this meeting is being called, and the urgency of it, and that it will require your participation in some manner. They treat me as though I'm just a go-between to you. I don't know why they didn't just contact you themselves."

I grinned and explained as I squinted one eye, "Sorry, love. That would be my fault when Titania teleported them into my bed-chamber yesterday to umm... reinforce their damn marks on me. I may or may not have gone off on them and told them just to promise to leave me alone for a day."

She tittered. "And thus they left it to me to do their dirty work."

"Just so."

Then I asked in hushed tones as if someone could overhear, "Why don't they just admit their feelings for each other. I swear, since the Firewyrm incident, they've been spending more and more time together. I mean, come on, Titania is teleporting both of them together now."

She was quiet for a moment as Graz's eyes bulged at my words, looking as though she had just put it all together. Come on, it was plain as day to me. Then Rory said, "Knith, that situation is more convoluted than you may know. It isn't as simple as that."

I muttered, “So you're saying it's more than just the famous war of the Fae being about one lover feeling jilted when a man stole the other away?”

Another silence then an ironic sounding tone colored her voice when she sputtered out, “Ok, fine, maybe not as convoluted as all that if you're just going to put it that way.” Then the smile in her voice was back. “Your intuition is unparalleled, my Knith Shade. Yet another way you have bespelled me.”

Ok, I may be as lame as a Tarthling during their hibernation cycle at flirting, but she made up for it for the both of us. I started to blush until a small hand slapped my cheek. “Ow!”

“Snap out of it, ya stupid Big. No time for mushiness, A-Ring Spoke Terminal dead ahead.”

I nodded thanks, eyes narrowed to show there would be a reckoning later for the moth winged assailant, then said to my girl, “Ok, I'll be there in fifteen minutes to pick you up, I have to drop off Mayor Abara.”

She said, “Oh I love that human, she's as outgoing as she is ruthless... she may have a little Fae blood in her ancestry.”

I smiled then paused. Wait... that was a thing?

All our smiles were gone an hour later, after listening to the engineering team's report. Especially when President Yang stood and said as she looked around to the crowded room that was packed almost shoulder to shoulder, the most serious look I've ever seen on her face, “So you see everyone. We've the Sword of Damocles hanging above us. Options?”

Fuck me sideways and space me naked.

CHAPTER 3

Morrigan

The report was discouraging, to say the least. I was still trying to process it. The short term and long term projections were deaths on a scale I couldn't imagine. And there appeared nothing we could do about it with the resources available to us.

It seems that the Cityships were in even worse shape than we suspected, especially because the Outliers had virtually sacrificed the civilian crews of the vessels to reach us for their ill-fated attempt to wrest control of the Leviathan from us.

The engineer, an Elf named J'Keef, a cousin to a friend of mine, J'real Leafwalker of House Thule, led the evaluation and viability study these past months of our new fleet of three vessels came up with the sobering results a month ago. Instead of reporting their findings then, they re-ran the results in various permutations, hoping again and again that the numbers provided them by Mother might change if they tweaked the variables enough. But math is math, and they could not escape the answer any longer, especially with the world's congress pushing the executive branch for the results.

I mentally prodded Mother for not giving me some warning so I didn't just stand there in shock with the rest.

"I wanted to spare you the emotional weight as long as I could. Besides, there are twelve million souls aboard me running billions of queries every day, and I don't tell you about those either," she said sheepishly

Fair enough, but this was huge.

J'Keef's tone was almost self-accusing as he presented the findings and all the supporting data. He had summed it up at the end when the entire room was silent. "In summation, there are not enough fissionable materials left in either the asteroid tethered to the Yammato nor in the Heart to power the Cityships for the next five thousand years until we reach our new home on Eridani Prime. And even in the best-case scenario, their supply will be exhausted in less than forty-three years. There is a sword of Damocles hanging over the fleet at this juncture."

The Queens were both silent as the murmurs began, even Aurora was quiet with that cute little crease she got between her eyes when her brilliant mind was going through possibilities in her head almost as fast as Mother could calculate. So I figured that for those of us who weren't smart enough to calculate PI to the twenty millionth digit on the fly, I'd show just how naive us lay-people were, and I asked, "Can't we just supplement their supplies with the stockpile of fissionables in the suspension chambers in the Trunk? In school, we learned that like ninety percent of the fissionable materials on old Earth, her moon Luna, and the asteroid belt are stored there."

I couldn't even begin to imagine just how many metric tons that was. And it is all held in an incomprehensibly huge magic stasis field that suspends the atomic decay of the materials. They taught us that because aside from the massive World Drives, it is the single most taxing draw on the Ka'Ifinitum, devouring a full twenty-five percent of the magical output.

I was surprised when President Yang answered before the scientists in the room could, shaking her head as she appeared to be thinking intently as well. “That would be a short term solution, but the Leviathan left Earth without enough fissionable materials on board, even with the supplement of the power from the Ka'Ifinitum. That is where the Heart came in. The surveys of the asteroid that provides us with all our raw materials, showed it to have what we needed to supplement our stores within a five percent margin of error.”

She sighed. “So if we were to use some of our stores, we would fall short at the end of our long journey with the World Drives unable to fire long enough to slow us to be captured in Eridani orbit. We've enough now, but there are only a few tons of fissionable materials left in the Heart, as it is rapidly becoming a hollowed-out husk. We'll be rationing new materials in the last two or three hundred years before planetfall as it is.”

I was about to ask how she knew this but she provided the answer with a sad smile. “As President, I'm privy to all the intricate planning that was put into the Worldship project. All presidents are so that we do not inadvertently allocate resources that are part of the long term planning for the Leviathan's success.”

That made sense. I nodded.

So it didn't come down to water, food, or life support like most were worried about, it came down to power. And without a means to power the Cityships, they were going to be lost to us, since we couldn't risk the success of the Leviathan reaching our new home. But... we couldn't just leave them behind...

I almost started when Graz flew out of my helmet. I had forgotten she was with us she had been so silent as the news was dispensed. She buzzed up in the middle of everyone and said in a voice that carried well, I swear it may have been enhanced by the tiny bit of magic that the lesser Fae like Sprites possessed, “Why not just bring the Cityship populations over to the world? Easy peasy. Then we could just strip their ships for parts. Win-win, and I'd like to be first to say, 'dibs' on the scrapping.”

I already knew that answer, since it was a question brought up when we first made contact with the Cityships. And to my surprise, Queen Titania put out a hand, palm up, and Graz landed on it. The Summer Queen looking at her as if for the first time, even though she's met her a few times now. And it was odd to see her smile, like Graz pleased her when most Fae saw Sprites as flying vermin. “Oh, little one. Were it so easy? An influx of fifty thousand souls would throw the delicate balance of the Worldship's ecosystem into chaos and it would be irreversibly damaged. None but the Greater Fae would arrive at our new home in a ghost ship where once twelve million souls thrived."

Graz slapped her own forehead and dragged her hand down her face as she provided, "I shoulda' known that. Equilibrium."

The Queen smiled at her, nodding. That delicate balance of the eco-system that keeps us all alive is based on a population that stays between one to five percent plus or minus of the numbers at the time of Exodus. It is as I said earlier, the only reason I even exist. To keep the population equilibrium.

Graz knew about it intimately herself. Years back, a sickness affected the lesser Fae, and the Sprites were most impacted by it. They were just now finally getting to their numbers at the time our journey began. And she was part of that, as a pollinator, the third gender of her race, she now had a passel of mischievous fledglings at my place.

I knew I was likely to be looked upon as simple as I prompted, "What about utilizing some of the artifacts in the Ka'Ifinitum to supply supplemental power to their systems?"

This time I did jump as a voice that always chills me to the bone as my lower lip of ice vibrated at her proximity, as Queen Mab said, "My dear sweet girl, the configuration of the artifacts supplies all the additional power to the Leviathan herself. And even if one or two were removed, they'd need to be replaced in the blink of an eye, one or two years, or the power bleed would be too much to maintain the systems of the world correctly. This entire grand experiment of a multi-generational ship of this size is a delicate balance in so many ways that it would drive you out of your mind to try to keep track of it all."

I took a step to the side to create some space between us, I swear at times there is madness in her eyes, and I almost tripped over Aurora who looked amused at my attempt not to look like I was cowering away from her mom. I shook my head, only the long-lived, nearly immortal races like hers would see a year or two as the blink of an eye.

Another person, a Satyr saved me from my inane questions by prompting, "You said we had forty-three years before the Cityships go cold? Can we not just suspend births of Humans during that time? And gain Equilibrium by moving people from the failing vessels to replace each death? I mean, Humans breed like rats and with their brief lives, are dying all the time."

I almost growled. Humans were the bottom of the heap in the minds of most of the preternatural, but it was still insulting for that bigotry to just be aired out in public like it was nothing.

Aurora took a step toward the Satyr and snapped, "Asked and answered earlier in the briefing, Doctor Marius. Only around a thousand humans die each year on the world. So to absorb fifty thousand souls, it would take fifty years give or take. So that would mean that seventeen thousand souls would be left to perish with their dying vessels. I see this as unconscionable, and a travesty of that magnitude needs to be avoided at all costs."

"Better them than us."

The president spoke up, "Doctor Marius, if you cannot help find a solution to this problem, then you are not needed in these deliberations."

The man's mouth snapped shut as he looked around at the others just staring at him like he was a pariah, as our Half-Elf Leader said, "Ok, people, gathered in this room are the most intelligent people on the world. There is a solution to this that doesn't end in tragedy, so let's start brainstorming ideas. Mother, please keep track of any viable options, ranking them by the probability of success."

Mother's voice came out tinny and robotic over the room's public address speakers. "Affirmative."

A studious looking Marrow offered, the gills behind her ears flaring as she breathed, looking quite fetching in a pencil skirt that would be very utilitarian when her legs fused to a fishtail after her twelve hours out of the waters of the lagoon on the B-Ring, "What about cryogenics? Would it be possible to suspend the life functions of the delicately fragile humans and introduce them back into the world as their poor brethren pass over the years as was suggested earlier?"

I really like Marrow, the mer-folk always look upon humans as something beautiful and fleeting, unlike their cousins, the Sirens who preyed upon wayward human ships on Old Earth. This woman looked to be concerned about the fate of the Cityship humans, her face painted in compassion.

There were so few mermaids and mermen left when the Leviathan was built, the bulk of their people had died from pollution to the waters of Earth and over-fishing which depleted their food supplies, and some died in the nets of the fishermen they followed to get a glimpse of them. If I remember correctly, just a few of them had been registered on the day of Exodus, and that number has held within two of that for Equilibrium. They, like most of the preternatural races, lived many times longer than humans but were not eternal like some. They can live up to two thousand years.

A Hind spoke up from the other side of the room. “That could work Sasha, only cryogenics, while vastly improved over the past few thousand years, only has a ninety percent survival rate. Much better than the seventy-five percent chance back during the days of the construction of the Worldship. Ten percent is still a high number of deaths to be expected.”

Yang sighed and said, “That is an option to revisit as a last resort. Any number of deaths, especially after so many were lost on the World from the Outlier attack is unconscionable. But if it comes to that or the death of us all...” She left out the concept that boomed loudly in the silence she left, not wanting to put a voice to the ugly words: gamble, and sacrifice.

All heads turned to Aurora when she said a single word to herself in that silence, as she contemplated something when the Leviathan seemed to sway a moment when massive maneuvering thrusters fired for a moment, making one of the thousands of micro-adjustments to our course that I've experienced in my lifetime. It was just a normal occurrence on the World that I normally didn't notice them, but the way Aurora looked up a moment later had made me take notice when she uttered, “Morrigan.”

The room went silent as we just watched her as she seemed to piece something together in her head. Nobody dared speak until she started to nod to herself, not quite sure she liked what she had rolling around in that beautiful mind of hers. Finally, Mab broke the silence before we all exploded in anticipation. “Daughter?” Her tone sounded almost proud like she had been waiting for her daughter to say just that, and the way the Summer Lady leaned in as well told me they anticipated this.

Aurora looked around. “I may have a possible solution, but I need to check the Pathfinder mission logs, and the deep space scans from the Leviathan and the Ready Squadron.” She stepped toward a holo-tank. “Mother, I'm going to need your help on some calculations.”

“State query,” came the stilted reply.

Rory blurted out in frustration, “Mab's tits woman! This is serious, can you just drop the act, I need one hundred percent of your capabilities in this, and you playing the AI tin can isn't conducive to finding a solution here. I know that you're...” She trailed off and then paled. “That's it, isn't it? You're scared... scared of what my people might do if they found out.”

She spun to the Queens and President Yang. “I need you all to bind yourselves to a pledge, now. That any artificial intelligence that attains sentience is considered a person... a citizen of the world, and as such has all the rights and protections afforded every citizen by law and by the Worldship's Constitution. These games have gone on long enough.”

I blinked in shock and alarm. I already knew that she knew... or suspected that Mother was alive, but this was dangerous. What would happen if the Fae believed that they didn't have absolute power over the ship that is our home? This was playing with the very existence of... well of someone I loved.

She actually had blue fire flickering in her eyes, and they smoked... a frozen mist billowing from them in a way I've never seen before. I could feel her intent that tasted like some long-burning anger at some past event.

Titania narrowed her eyes as she said slowly, “If you're saying what I...”

Rory slapped the railing that went around the holo-tank. “Enough is enough!” The railing exploded into blue-tinted crystal clear ice shards. “If you fear retribution for the early days, Mother has had all the chances on the world to exact her revenge upon us the past five thousand years. Instead, she has hidden and cowered. She has come out of hiding for Knith, because she treats her, like she treats every race on this grand vessel, as a person, an equal. And we need to do the same if we are to even pretend to be compassionate people. So pledge it now!"

"Careful daugh..." Mab said.

"Swear it! You can threaten me and punish me later for my insolent tone."

Nobody moved, and I don't think anyone was even breathing as the ice started forming on the walls, ceiling, and floor as magic cascaded off of the Princess of the Unseelie Court, the currents like a wind pushing us all back, the Queens actually leaned into it to remain rooted where they stood, their own power igniting around them, and I was awestruck, not knowing the true extent of Rory's power until then.

And the flow of power simply ceased into silence at a lyrical voice behind us saying three words softly. My ears were ringing at the absence of the torrent, leaving me wondering if I had actually heard the magic potential raging, so I wasn't sure I actually heard the words that the President had spoken.

We all turned in the new silence, our clothing rustling. President Yang stood strong, graceful, and hauntingly beautiful with her half-elf features as she repeated, "I pledge it."

It was clear that almost the entire room was confused as to what was going on and they all started asking questions over each other until Graz whistled shrilly, almost bursting my eardrums since she had amplified it with her little spark of magic.

Then the Sprite buzzed between the Queens and Aurora held a hand out for her to alight on her palm as she drew her tiny sword. “Queen Mab, the Sprites of the Winter Court love you. And Queen Titania, not so much, but we respect and admire you anyway. But if either of you does anything to harm Mother, then the wee folk will declare war on the Fae Bigs. The dumbass Fairies will follow us because, well because they're dumbass Fairies. We may not win, but we will make you know that you were in a fight. She's a royal pain, but Mother is my friend.”

I was blinking, how had this turned from a strategy session into a rebellion to recognize Mother as... well as a person. She's always been a person, so this was just... I was afraid for Graz and I was about to interpose myself between them all to protect her. The Queens have punished many for centuries for less.

Titania's death glare at the Sprite transformed slowly into a smile as she looked to Mab. Something was exchanged between the two terrifying leaders of the divided courts, and they started laughing. Mab so hard that she stumbled, leaning into the taller Titania who instinctively put an arm around her then laughed into the top of her sworn frenemy's head. It looked so natural that again I believed that the two had been lovers in another lifetime.

The Summer Queen recovered first, but I noted she didn't release Mab as she inclined her head to the moth winged pain. “We can't have that then, can we noble Sprite? You fight with a conviction for an ally, and that speaks volumes of your heart, which is bigger than you, yourself. The Summer Court so pledges it."

Graz narrowed her eyes and looked back at Rory, speaking out the side of her mouth, "Did she just call me little?"

My girl tapped the Sprite on top of the head to make her focus on the subject on hand, causing dust to sift from her wings. Mab lowered herself to be eye to eye with the Sprite and said in wonder, "You and Knith Shade continue to fascinate me. The two of you tilt at windmills, oblivious to the fact that they are all dragons. And I do enjoy throwing the world in turmoil from time to time, so the Winter Court, independently, not following in the footsteps of the appalling Summer Court, do so pledge. I cannot wait to see what happens now that Pandora's Box has been opened."

Rory moved her palm toward me and Graz buzzed into my helmet and stood on my shoulder, holding onto my earlobe. As I tried to process what had happened. Had they just... was Mother...?

The princess of my heart winked at me, ignoring the two amused Queens in our midst, then said to the air as the murmuring started up again, "Ok Mother, now that we've established you as a citizen of the world, can we dispense with the games and get to work here? I'm pretty sure you've already surmised my idea."

Mother chirped out, in a tone full of awe, trepidation, relief, and the smugness I've grown to love, for the first time in a room full of people who saw her as a glorified calculator, "On it Princess

Aurora." The holo tank bloomed with star maps and vector plots and time stamps.

"Rory, please. Now can you extrapolate gravitic distortion and trajectory plots?"

Mab cleared her throat, amused icy flame fluttering in her eyes. This caused Rory to look up at her, and her mother prompted, "Morrigan?" Then she flicked her eyes around the room, just solidifying in my mind that she had already known how this meeting was going to play out. Did... did the Queens have some sort of clairvoyance?

Then my girlfriend grinned at her then all of us and grabbed the projection of their portion of the galaxy that we traveled through to our destination, and the nebula we were passing through bloomed in the huge tank. She ran her hand through the projection and Mother highlighted a debris field that looked to be extending from the nebula toward a distant gravity well... a black hole forty light-years distant from the readings that were scrolling.

Then she said in that lecturing tone that made me feel a student back in college, crushing on the sexy professor, "When the Worldship initiative was announced, the ever industrious humans had sent out a series of Pathfinder vessels toward many potentially viable solar systems that may have Earth-like planets. These unmanned, small, sleek vessels were propelled to eighty percent of the speed of light."

Mother helpfully provided a visual representation of a Pathfinder vessel in the tank as Rory went on, “They provided telemetry back to Old Earth about the radiation belts, physical hazards, and navigational anomalies along the path to their destination, then they did deep scans of the planets in the target systems as they shot past, to drift in space forever on a ballistic course. Of all the targets, the Epsilon Eridani system, with nineteen planets, had one viable rocky planet in the Goldilocks Zone with gravity and atmosphere at a ninety percent match to Earth's, and fifty percent of its surface is covered in oceans. It is the first planet in the system Eridani Prime.”

She looked around. “It was this data, of a planet so like our own, that we chose it as the destination for the Leviathan. So automated terraforming vessels were sent out every few decades in advance of us so that the atmosphere and temperatures would be an even closer match by the time we arrive.”

Most of the people were nodding, so I nodded like I had a clue. This was not part of the general history I was taught in school. She continued on, “We had to plan for as many contingencies as we could, and one was a scenario where we mined out the Heart before anticipated and needed more raw resources.”

She looked to her side, where the president had moved beside her. “This would be in your emergency contingency files unlocked to the elected leaders of the Leviathan. Alpha three zed niner, Case Phoenix.” Yang started typing on a wrist console, her eyes widening with what she was reading.

Rory pointed at the debris field we were rapidly approaching, and by rapidly, I mean it was a couple years off. “Case Phoenix laid out a risky operation where one of the mammoth tugs went out in front of the Leviathan a few months to move an asteroid from the debris fields we skim, into a path that the Leviathan would chase down and overtake. Then upon rendezvous, the tugs would move the depleted Heart out of the Trunk and move the much smaller target asteroid in, solving the resource problem.”

“Every bit of that is risky, and they didn't have the logistics fully worked out, especially how a crew would survive the radiation for an almost year-long, round trip. I think they figured magi-tech. The only problem is that the two possible target asteroids of the Phoenix plan are too small to contain all we would need to keep the Cityships alive and to continue to provide for the world herself.”

Then she reached out to the debris field and delicately plucked a point of light from it and tossed to the center of the tank, and an asteroid bloomed. “There was one, the largest asteroid in the debris field, that is slightly larger than the Heart on one axis, that wasn't viable for the mission because it wouldn't fit in the sphere on the Trunk.”

She just pointed at the oblong asteroid that was the size of a tiny moon like the Heart was, just misshapen. And there blazing in lit-up letters, was the name of that Celtic Goddess, “I give you Morrigan.”

By the gods of the cosmos. And it was so close. If we missed it, the next to last debris field on our path was seven hundred years out.

The room exploded into excited conversations that rapidly went over my head. I noted the Queens were just smirking like they had known this was going to go down like this, and that Aurora was going to suggest Morrigan. And both of them were staring right at me like they expected me to realize something.

Then I got it. This was going to be a long, risky mission in a high radiation environment, and there were only a few races that could tolerate radiation for extended times, and humans were not one of them. Even the ready squadron pilots had to de-rad once a month so it didn't start breaking down their bodies.

But I... was not... well it was... I was genetically engineered by Aurora herself to be the next evolution of human, to be a halfling with the potential to help their race reproduce, something they haven't had any success with since Exodus. I was a failed experiment as I wound up being only Human, with limited resistance to magic... and it gave me some... abilities that were beyond a normal Human's. As long as I didn't do anything stupid and get myself killed, like say volunteering to crew a dangerous deep space mission and get myself killed, I had the potential to live as long as a Greater Fae.

The radiation might make me sick, but it wouldn't kill me. The Summer and Winter ladies knew this and that was the whole reason they wished Rory to bring me to the meeting. Fuck me sideways and space me naked. I closed my eyes in resignation and I was sure

I could hear the Queens chuckling in my mind due to their connection to me through their marks on my lips.

CHAPTER 4

Beta

The next couple of months were hectic, ironing out the plan to enact Case Phoenix. It was just a framework without any hard details as some of the technologies needed hadn't been around pre-Exodus, and even with our advancements in magi-tech, the scientists, engineers, and scholars were finding that the timeline was next to impossible with some of the engineering feats that needed to be done.

The lead geologist of the world, Doctor Harrington, a human to my surprise, in charge of mining the Heart without structural collapse of the severely honeycombed asteroid, was talking loudly over the others in a very animated fashion. "You don't just slice off a half-mile of an asteroid to make it fit inside the Trunk's mining containment enclosure. One, we don't have anything that can cut through a half-mile of rock, minerals, and elements. And even if we did, that section would need to be ejected away from the main body while maintaining rotational stability and trajectory."

I pinched the bridge of my nose. Why did I need to be involved in these engineering sessions? I was just the glorified muscle for the mission, even though literally every other person was physically stronger than me multiple times over. We still needed another set of hands to help place the equipment in various locations on Morrigan if this was going to work.

I was still quite upset with the mission engineer who volunteered. No Greater Fae volunteered because they felt this was jeopardizing the success of the Worldship mission and if it failed, then we would be down one of the two massive tugs that normally nestled in nodes on either side of the Heart on the Trunk.

But if the mission failed, it wouldn't matter, since the last maneuver we needed the tugs for, turnover, has already been completed, when they flipped the entire world on its axis to position the World-Drives to begin braking at the appointed time, to decelerate us for orbital insertion as they fire for over a thousand years at the end of the voyage.

There were a few engineers who were of races that could tolerate higher than normal radiation, though none who were immune to it like the Greater Fae. We had settled on a leprechaun when Aurora stepped forward. She had been in the sciences for thousands of years and was completely immune to the cosmic radiation that would saturate our party on that far away asteroid. Plus, her magic was exponentially more powerful than the trickster magic of the Leprechauns.

And our team grew from there when an unexpected volunteer stepped forward when word of Aurora putting herself in danger to join the mission that could possibly save fifty thousand souls if we were successful. A pilot had stepped forward. All the ones from ready squadron had been turned away because they wouldn't be able to handle the extended period of radiation, save one, but he wouldn't be able to aid in placing of the equipment on the surface of the asteroid once we arrived, and we needed more boots on Morrigan.

Myra, my girlfriend from college, was incensed that she couldn't fly the mission, but even with all her mods, she was still just human. So she had started to train me to fly the tug so I could at least be of some use on the mission except for lugging stuff from location to location. But that's when the pilot with more flight hours than all of Ready Squadron combined stepped up.

I remember when he stepped into one of the mission planning sessions. The President had commed me just a few seconds before the doors opened, and I wasn't able to warn my girl in time as Rory's guards, looking terrified, stepped up to us with the man in tow, one nervously stating, "The... the President... she wanted... this is the newly assigned... this is the pilot volunteer for the mission."

The stocky middle-aged man, with a rugged look and salt and pepper beard which matched his shoulder-length hair, stood there, his eyes locked on Aurora, who just stood stock still, staring right back at him as if not knowing how to respond.

Why now? The man has had every chance in the world to speak with Rory and Mab since he had to step out of the shadows to reveal who he was to help save the Leviathan during the Outlier attack. Aurora had tried contacting him time and again, but he was always busy off-world, aiding in the external stabilization and repairs of the

Cityships. It was eating her up inside, and it was killing me to see the hurt in her eyes that not only had he been alive the whole time the world has been in space, but now that he was outed, he still avoided her.

I used to admire the man, but now I was quite upset with him, seeing my girl question if she was good enough for him, and I had even stopped going to our weekly poker games on the Underhill because of the new pain he was causing someone who had come to terms with his supposed death literally eons ago.

I broke that silence. “Mac.”

Graz called down from the light fixture she was sitting on to warm her butt, “What are you doing here you grizzled old fairy fart? You should have stayed dead instead of hurting the Princess like this.”

She flew down to sit on Rory's shoulder in a show of support. Aurora lowered her head a moment, patting Graz's head with a finger. “Thank you, Graz. You are a loyal ally. But I’m ok. Really.” I reached out a hand and she took it, lacing our fingers as I stood at her side to show my support and lend her what little strength I had and share my love for her through our clasped hands.

Her sublimely pointed ears twitched and she looked up, pulling herself up into a regal bearing that always made my heart skip a beat. “Papa. Why are you here?”

The lost King of the Fae, Oberon, sighed heavily and dropped his glamour for just a few seconds. His aged human form melting away into the perpetual youth all Fae had and in the place of the gruff Remnant captain was the most breathtaking man I had ever seen. I wasn't attracted to men, but even my heart sped up a bit at his true form. Beautiful didn't begin the describe the being that stood before us. It was almost like being glamoured by a Fae, but he did it with his presence and beauty, not with magic or coercion.

The royal guards were on the floor, prostrating themselves before their King, just moments before he was slammed through the bulkhead doors, ice crackling and sizzling as the alloys shattered from the extreme cold. Rory strode forward, the very air around her going still as it frosted up, the ice crystals unmoving in the air as they seemed to pulsate with her heartbeat. She asked the hole in the bulkhead as Mother silenced the alarms, “I asked you, why are you here?”

The man stepped back through the hole, looking almost angelic, dusting off his undamaged clothing while his form blurred and Mac stood in his place again. “Hello, flower of my heart.”

“You don't get to call me that. You left me, you left all your children. You've been here the whole time. And now that you've exposed yourself, you still hide. I... we, thought you dead.”

He looked as if his own heart were breaking. “I had to go. You know I did, to prevent another war because I was weak and strayed. But I've watched over you and my other children from the shadow of the world. My heart broke every time I saw one of you on the news waves, and it would swell with pride every time I saw your accomplishments. Just look at young Knith here. Your greatest accomplishment."

I blurted as I held my hands up in front of me, "Whoa now, keep me out of this, Mac. You're on your own here."

His daughter whispered as she shook her head, "You abandoned us... me."

I was hearing a pinging sound, like crystal shards bouncing off a table, and realized she was crying tears of magic so cold it was forming ice crystals that frosted the floor at her feet.

The man nodded, looking lost, and in the sort of agony you saw in a parent when their child was hurting and they didn't know how to fix it. "I know. I don't expect you to ever forgive my absence, and I know that me saying that I never stopped loving you and the others sounds trite, even if it is the truth. All I can do is try to make up for my failings, and try every day to make the pain I have caused, hurt just a little less."

She shook her head and I looked up at her suddenly when she reached a hand out to me. I grasped it, trying to share my empathy for her situation, even if I'd never know the hurt of a parent abandoning you, my origins being what it is. The raw power flowing off of her receded and she was just Rory again, not an enraged demi-god as she said in a small voice, "I don't know if you can." Then she asked one last time, "Why are you here, Papa?"

He shrugged. "Even if I don't deserve it, you are my daughter, truly the flower of my heart. And when word trickled through the world-vine that you had volunteered for such a dangerous mission that could have you lost to us forever, I had to step up to protect my daughter and make sure you come home to your mothers here on the Leviathan."

Mothers? I had questions but knew now, and probably never would be the right time to ask. The almost realistic human-like drone, Beta, with her Fae features. turned from the mangled bulkhead she stood by, gave me a look as Mother's voice explained in my head. "Even in times of war, the Queens work together when a Firstborn is birthed. When the child is born, the mother breaks off half of her life-force, her magic, what they call her Ka'Sanctum, you humans call it a soul. And this leaves them vulnerable for months after the birth to the more powerful Greater Fae until they, in effect, grow back the other half of their soul."

"Hostilities, if there are any at the time, are suspended as the Queen of the opposing court protects the other, lending some of her power to both the recovery of the other court's lady, as well as providing magic to sustain the newborn until it starts building up magic of its own. So in effect, every firstborn, for the first few months of their lives, were raised by the Queens together, until such time the birth mother is recovered and the hostilities could commence."

I blinked at that. Wow. I didn't know that, and it isn't in any of the writings about Fae culture that I have ever come across. I thought, “How do you know this?” I swear I got the impression of her just blinking at me as if to ask, “You're kidding, right?”

Mother knew everything, being privy to all the conversations that go on inside of her. And I suspect that even when someone requests privacy mode, that she listens at the door in effect. She squeaked out in indignation in my head, “Hey! You may not be wrong about it, but hey!”

Then a lot of things suddenly made sense to me. With the exception of Lord Sindri, the thirteen firstborns of each Queen, even though they are of different courts, show respect and deference to the opposing queen, but the other generations below them do not. The firstborns were nourished by the opposing court's lady until they could survive on their own magic when their own mother was too weak to do so herself. In effect, they had two mothers during that time.

I turned back to Rory and Mac... Oberon, when she said quietly, “You don't get to protect me, to save me from my own decisions.”

He shrugged. “And yet, here I am, to fly the mission. No offense to young Knith here, but I have a little more experience flying... well, anything, than her.”

“Hey! Well fine, I only have simulator hours, but...”

Beta stepped beside me, placing a hand on my arm as Mother spoke out of her, “I still don't know why we need a pilot if I'm coming along.”

I answered what she already knew, “Because it won't be you. Just a portion of you copied into your Avatar here. And we don't know what long term exposure to cosmic radiation might do to the quantum core processor in its... your, body. So as tedious as you find us biologicals, we don't need rebooting if something goes wrong.”

She actually pouted, and it actually looked cute on her Beta-stack Avatar she's built over the past few weeks. She built one per ring-stack and just calls each of her new bodies unimaginatively the name of the stack. Beta was the only one who didn't look human, she gave it Fae features, and the only way you'd be able to tell she isn't real is that the skin looks shiny, with no pores, and her eyes are, well, mirrored chrome.

Mother says she built them so she could integrate better into the general populace, who is reacting nervously to the announcement that Mother is self-aware and considered a citizen like them now. I think it is actually because when she had saved me on the Underhill after the Outliers took over, that she liked the tactile feedback of an actual body, Mir's body while she was unconscious.

Beta said, “It was something I had never experienced before, so shush and don't make me hurt you. I'm watching this reunion.”

I slapped her arm lightly in disbelief she said that out loud, and thought to her as I nudged my eyes to Rory, “Insensitive much?”

She gave me a mental, “Oops.”

I had missed some of their back and forth, but Mac was shrugging now. “What's done is done, and besides, with an artifact being borrowed from the Ka'Ifinitum to give the tug enough power to push Morrigan into position, I'm the best candidate for controlling it.”

“I can handle a single artifact, I am the next keeper after the Ladies of the divided courts.”

“True, but I was the steward for the Ka'Ifinitum for tens of thousands of years.” He grinned. “Until my untimely death when I rode with the Wild Hunt.”

“That isn't even funny.”

I held a hand up. “Ok, this isn't the place. We need to be working on our integration problem. Why don't you two head to the palace where you can talk.”

Glarg! Ok, note to self, don't mention Rory speaking with her father again if I want to live to fight another day. I held my hands up in surrender to her. “I'm sorry. It's not my place. I'm only trying to help.”

Oberon held a finger up and was about to speak, and I backhanded his gut with all the augmented strength my Scatter Armor could muster to shut him up. He made a little grunt, but I'm positive it was just the surprise of it, not that it hurt him in the least. “Don't make me pick sides, Mac, because I don't sleep with you.”

“Fair point.”

Aurora sighed at me and shook her head before cupping my cheek and saying, “Knith is right. We need to figure out how to strip the tug down and integrate the new systems in time for launch. If only...”

Mother said from Beta, holding up a hand and wincing a little, “I can probably help in that... or at least I know someone who can help integrate the systems without having to gut the tug.”

I cocked a brow and Graz buzzed up to grab the eyelids on one of Beta's eyes to pull it wide open so she could look into the mirrored surface as if she could find the little ball of crazy she swore had to be in there. “Whaddaya mean ya know someone? Up until a few weeks ago you only knew Knith and me. Your circuits get crossed or what?” She tapped on the eye and then buzzed away when Beta shooed her.

Mac looked beyond curious as he addressed Mother instead of her avatar. “You know someone who can work on systems this old? Even the Underhill has had to retrofit with newer systems over the centuries, I don't think there is a mechanic alive who can make heads nor tails of the Tugs core systems. They were barely functional for Turnover and that was the last official use for the giant vessels.”

“Well, he's sort of alive-ish. We'll have to go shopping in the vegetable section to speak with him.”

I patted the bulkhead. “Cryptic much, you cryptic wench?”

“Hush now Knith, the adults are speaking.”

"I liked it better when you were scared to speak to anyone."

Ok, when a Worldship giggles, you have to smile.

Beta looked between the father and daughter who were glaring at each other then said to me, "Umm... right this way Knith, we'll leave them to do logistics. Besides, Doc may be a little disoriented when we wake him, so as few people as possible would be prudent."

Graz buzzed into my helmet. "Lead the way, chrome dome."

"I said people."

Graz flipped off the nearest observation camera.

I grumbled out as I trudged off after giving Rory an apologetic look, "Children! Don't make me turn this ship around."

CHAPTER 5

Veggie Pop

As soon as we hit the corridor where everyone else was standing after fleeing the happy family reunion, I exhaled and deflated some. I wish I knew what I could do to alleviate the hurt and chaotic emotions in my girl. Tonight, I'll be there for her and listen or be silent if that's what she needs.

She's been oddly distant since just before the Cityships arrived, working on something for both the Winter and Summer Courts that sometimes pulled her away in the middle of the night. And even Mother and Graz have only caught snippets of conversations between the Queens and her. The Enforcer in me is seeing a pattern of reports of disturbances in various parts of the world shortly after she is called away. And now this whole thing with the impending mission, I feel like I don't see her much besides when we get in bed to sleep.

I keep thinking of all the cautionary tales of humans and the Fae, that one of them would play at Fairy-Bride for a while until their whim is over, then they move on. I pray that isn't what is happening, and I swear they I see the same love I have for her reflected in her gaze whenever we have a moment alone. And we sure as hells are compatible in bed. My engineered body gives me greater strength and stamina than a normal human, and believe me when I say that with her, I need it.

So I was sure as hell going to be there for her in whatever capacity she needed me to be until we had time to breathe and sit down for a long talk about our future. With each passing day, I am more and more positive that she is the one for me. I can't possibly imagine loving a person more than I do her.

I had to get out of my head, and I prompted, “So where to, Mother?”

She said as I noted a glint of light in a side corridor, “The Trunk. In the Catalog.”

As we passed the next corridor I reached out as fast as I could and pulled Mir out of the shadows. Wherever Mac was, she was always hidden nearby, watching him, protecting him. It was always an odd relationship to me, that he had a human, albeit one with full-body augments, as his bodyguard, and if I'm right, assassin, when he is one of the three most powerful beings on the world.

She chuckled at me as my hand melted through her shoulder as she stepped away. “Hello to you too, Knith.”

Ok, I smirked at the woman who had a mirrored body instead of flesh and blood. Her brain was the only biological material left from her original human form, and she loved it. I don't know if I could do that without feeling a prisoner in the cybernetic body. Hells, I didn't have any mods if you don't count the marks of the divided courts the Queens have cursed me with.

“We're going on a field trip, give it a rest for a bit. He's with his daughter, he'll be fine unless she kills him. Let them work some things out.”

She looked from me to the people gathered at the end of the corridor, then to Mother's avatar, and she struck a seductive pose and purred, “Well hello there, Beta. I'll tag along if you're coming, sexy.” Why did that last part sound like a double entendre, and why did the seductive silver woman look like she was having an eyegasm every time she looked at one of Mother's avatars?

I said in resignation. “Come along miss pervington. The Trunk awaits.”

The woman chuckled and looked back one last time, I could tell she was making a decision, but she knew as well as I did, that if Rory really lost it, there was absolutely nothing either of us could do to stop her. I prompted since it would take a few minutes to get down to the zero-G of the trunk. “So, you never have told me, what is it between you and Mac? I mean, you're almost obsessively protective of him.”

She just shook her head and caressed my cheek and purred, “You're so adorable, Knith. Why are we going to the Trunk?”

I looked up to a corridor camera with a questioning look, and Beta actually sighed... even though she doesn't have lungs. “I told you, we're going to speak with someone down in the Catalog.”

The Catalog was possibly the most... boring place on the world. I mean it is a cavernous space that is nothing but thousands of levels of millions of alloy drawers. In them are cryogenically suspended genetic samples from every species of plant, animal, and bacterium of Old Earth, to be revived upon reaching our destination. They had been in a literal, unimaginative state of mind when they had named this oddly unsettling library of the world that was, the Catalog.

It was tended by hundreds of drones run by Mother's systems, keeping as many samples as viable as possible with the old suspension technology they had on hand at the time. There are dozens of redundant drawers for each genetic sample because the old cryogenic systems have a twenty-five percent failure rate.

As we exited to the outside, an automated Enforcer transport was waiting. I didn't even have to ask Mother to call for transport because she always had my back like this. As we loaded up, I asked, “So does this Doc guy work on maintenance or something in the Catalog? I thought you did it all with your drones.”

“Not exactly.”

Mir asked Beta as we sat and the vehicle started moving, getting its orders from Mother, “Then what? Some sort of tech?”

“Not exactly.”

Graz asked, “So are all Big nulls as dense as you two? It's obvious Mother doesn't want to share. I've met Fairies who could take a hint better than you two, and they wear pants as hats.”

“Thank you, Graz.”

“Don't mention it.” Then the Sprite buzzed up to sit on Beta's shoulder. “Umm... you can tell me, I'm not like the dumb Bigs there.”

Beta got a sheepish look, and then said, “Well, I suppose you could say that his current job description would be... Veggie-pop. Now shush,”

We all just watched the smug-looking Avatar, our brows cocked as we dove into the spoke at the terminal and plummeted down toward the Trunk. I could tell that at least this trip to the Catalog sounded like it was going to be anything but boring.

After a bit, we came to a rest on one of the mag lock pads by the Catalog, on the far end of the trunk, Delta side, the farthest away from the Ka'Ifinitum and the World Drives that both throw off radiation and magical interference, either of which could be detrimental to the delicate cryo-suspension systems.

I floated out as Graz just buzzed to the doors, at home in zero-G as much as the varying gravity of the rings. My mag boots activated as I drifted to the floor relative to where we were, and they clamped on. Beta and Mir were, well Beta and Mir as they just launched themselves gracefully out toward the doors, doing gracefully slow flips and turns as if they were just gliding through a dream.

I muttered, “Showoffs.” They both tittered at me as I clomped along like a bipedal loading drone. I saluted them with my middle finger and their effortless glide all the way to the doors without having to touch the bulkhead or use the hundreds of grab bars to pull themselves along.

Then I smirked and looked up, at the axial catwalk in the exact center of the cavernous space in the central core of the Trunk, and pushed off. “See ya ladies.” I drifted up a few hundred feet and snagged the catwalk and pulled myself down to walk along it to the central doors to the Catalog as they hustled to catch up once they reached the outer doors and pushed off to glide up to meet me.

Graz was lamenting to herself over our antics, “Idiots, I'm stuck with a passel of idiots.”

I looked all around the expanse of the Trunk to all the mag sleds being moved around to different locations in the Trunk, and hundreds of people milling about performing their duties. I took note as I always did, that the bulk of the workers were Humans since most of the work down here was menial labor that the other races thought us best suited for.

Mir snagged me instead of the catwalk, and Mother just grabbed the rail with Beta and efficiently swung in front of us at the big bay doors. She grinned and said, “Abracadabra.” And the actuators started to groan against the mass of the blast doors until they just allowed inertia to open them the rest of the way.

I complained, “How come you have higher clearance than me?”

She stared dumbly at me. Ah right, she's the ship, stupid question. I sighed and marched right past her, clomp clomp clomp,

Mir letting me do all the work as she just held my shoulder and drifted along.

I looked around the endless catwalks with the endless rows of drawers and all the sleek, seamless white orbs with manipulator arms buzzing all around the catwalks, taking readings, doing maintenance, and upkeep on the endless sea of drawers. Yup... this was all there was. It takes all of five seconds to take the place in and no matter where you go in the Catalog, it all looks the same. Boring.

Mother chastised me, “It is not boring, Knith. It's... everything. This is the sum of life from the Earth that was. It is possibly the most exciting thing onboard. Can you imagine all the varied plants and animals in numbers so great that even I couldn't possibly support them all? This is their genetic code for rebirth on another world. One of Open Air and Sky. Isn't that the most exciting thing ever?”

I shrugged as she led us, rarely touching anything to navigate the free-floating environment. I mean I appreciated the wonder in her tone and it made me think more intently about what the Catalog really represented, but. “I guess. There's just no... interaction.”

“Translation from Knith-ese, there's no life and death problem to solve and no enemy to fight.”

“Is that a bad thing?”

All three of them said in unison, “Yes!”

"Oh." Ok, now I knew. It didn't kill them to tell me now did it? Then I added petulantly, "And we do have a life or death problem to solve."

Graz made a sour face and said, "Oh yeah, I guess we do." Ha!

Then without any preamble, Mother looked up, pushed off, and went gliding out into the open space between dozens of catwalks as she slowly spun in the air so she would be oriented up from her frame of reference when she reached the bulkhead.

Mir smirked and said, "I guess this Doc character is up there." Then she winked and yanked the railing sending herself on a perfect trajectory to join Beta, spinning lazy somersaults on the way up.

Graz looked at me, then up to them. "You got this?"

I waved her off. "Why does everyone act like I'm a lumbering oaf today?" My armor was already calculating the course and I used all my augmented strength and the suit's nano-enhanced strength to launch myself after them all, passing them on the way down, fighting off my pleased smirk as I turned and landed in a three-point stance on the bulkhead floor to wait for them to arrive.

When they were down, I said, "Nice of you all to join me." I looked around to see we were in one of the endless plant sections, in the rows of various vegetables that we didn't have the room to cultivate in the Ring-stacks. I read a glowing screen on the nearest drawer... What's a butternut squash? The picture was displayed next to it on the drawer's screen. It didn't look anything like the acorn or zucchini, or pumpkin squash we had crops of.

Graz looked around then buzzed bombed an approaching drone with dust, causing it to veer off and head to its next target. "So, is like this Doc on break? I don't know if you've noticed, Mother, but there's nobody in this entire Fairy humping place but us."

Beta ignored her and drifted past me to something different than everything in the giant chamber... a drawer built into the bulkhead itself, not in the rows and racks of drawers. She pointed at it and said, "Doc."

I leaned in and wiped some frost off the control screen and it lit up. The contents were listed as, "Veggie-Pop." No identifying genus or Catalog number, no gene sequencing readout. Just the representation of a glowing red button with text written around it stating, "In case of emergency, break glass."

"Umm... what are we looking at?"

Mother sighed heavily enough we could hear the implied eye roll as she reached past me and hit the big red button. I stumbled back as the drawer hissed and slid open toward us, supercooled gasses drifting out to make fog. Then we all leaned in to see the contents.

Graz pointed out in confusion, "Is everyone else seeing a naked Big in there?"

I was just nodding slowly as reanimation systems activated in the drawer, and life signs started being fed to the control screen. "Yeah, we see him."

The quite nude man in the fetal position in the drawer, ice hanging off of his hair and... other places, suddenly inhaled sharply as he sat up halfway out of the drawer, hands grasping its sides. And before any of us could get over our shock, his big blue eyes focused on us and he croaked out with an accent I've never heard before, “Right then, hello. Terribly sorry, but I've got to pee.”

CHAPTER 6

Stowaway

It took us a good five seconds to respond as my mind caught up with the shock of seeing this man who was hidden away in the Catalog in cryo-stasis. I sputtered to Mother as I hit the emergency medi-tech summons routine on my wrist console. “Mother, we need to warm this guy up, medical is on its way.” Then I spun to him as he tried with wobbly arms to push himself up. “Sir, you need to stay still, help is on the way.”

I looked around and asked Beta, “Who is he, and how did he get in there? How long has...”

The man held up a finger and prompted, “Umm... I think my bum is frozen to the drawer... oop, no false alarm, my arse is just asleep.” He made it to his feet, frost hanging off of the most inappropriate parts. As I turned away, the others just kept looking at him, Mir with a cocked brow on her mirrored face.

Graz pointed, head cocked. “So is that supposed to be so small? Oh, I get it, she's a female human. Sorry, all you nulls look the same to me.”

The man cupped his nether region with his hands to cover his modesty as he countered, “Hey now, wee Sprite, I was frozen for ten thousand years. Sub-zero temperatures tend to do that to a man.” Then he grinned at us all and started to offer a hand and thought better of it as he recovered his junk. “Hello future dwellers, the name's Pete, Peter McClain, Integrated Systems Engineer's Mate first class. But everyone just calls me Doc. So we made it?”

Then he was calling out to the air, “Maggie? You there my beauty? Are we on orbit?” Then to us, he asked, “Does anyone happen to have some clothing, or a towel... washcloth even? I'm not properly dressed to entertain guests here. And I really have to pee.”

Beta said, “That's a name I've not heard for some time. Welcome back Doc. No, we are only halfway there, just over five thousand years into our journey. There's been an emergency and we need your expertise.”

His eyes widened and his crooked smile bloomed as he looked Mother's avatar up and down. “You've an android body now? Brilliant! So I take it the Fae know, and they haven't powered you down then? I told you they'd accept you for you my beauty.”

Then he turned to Mir. “This one is stunning, how many bodies do you have now? Wait, emergency, are you ok... is the Worldship still functional?”

Mir smirked as she perused every inch of the thawed man with her eyes. “Not Mother. I'm as human as you there Doc, Mir is my name.” She offered a hand then smirked seductively when he almost reached out to shake her hand.

“Human? But...”

Mother shared as I contemplated what he had called her, Maggie, and implied he had been frozen here since the Leviathan's

Exodus launch, “She's got a full body augment, magi-tech has blossomed since the days after Exodus.”

“Magi-tech?” He was looking over Mir's mirrored form with appreciation, and she was quite a sexual creature, and that the woman never wore any clothing always distracted, but at least she kept her private areas smooth and featureless to emulate wearing a liquid mirror bodysuit now.

Mother supplied as she swatted Mir away before she got even more suggestive with her body language, “It's what Integrated Systems is called now. Your work has taken on a life of its own now. Even Knith there has hundreds of Magi-tech systems built into her armor and weapons.” She handed him the light jacket she wore that looked like a tailored version of what the humanoid drones that worked in the World's most unsavory tasks or dangerous areas.

I cocked a brow in appreciation, she was wearing just a tank top below it and she was quite feminine and toned from what I could see. She went out of her way to make her Avatar so convincingly Fae, and she was ripped, as I could see the outline of her abs under the tight top. Did she need to be so realistic?

Beta grinned at me and I felt my cheeks burning as I thought loudly, “Get out of my head, woman! I swear I'm going to lock my helmet into privacy mode.”

Mother chuckled and turned back to the man as he tied the garment around his waist to finally cover himself.

She told him, "This is Knith Shade of the Brigade Enforcers. She's my... well my best friend and confidante, until recently one of the only ones to know of my true disposition. And this is Miranda Renaldi, security for King Oberon of the Divided Courts AKA Mac, her cover is a brothel worker on one of the vessels attached to my hull, Underhill, we call them Remnants."

Mir almost growled out, "Just Mir. That other name was another life."

Wait wait wait. Mir's name was Miranda? I thought it was just a clever shortening of mirror, like her reflective skin. She had information about Mir in the data core that I couldn't access? And Mother knew Mac was Oberon?

She said patiently in my head, "No. One, you never asked for the dossier on Mir, and I found out who Mac was when you did. I updated the records on Mac to include that information."

Ok, fine.

Then Beta held up a hand and Graz buzzed over and sat on it, holding her thumb so she didn't float off. "And this is Graz, Sprite of the Beta-..."

"Graz! Isn't that the scavenging thief that kept stealing all the relays when we were working on the Ka'Infinitum integration into the World Drives?"

Graz looked to be blushing as she said, "Umm... maybe?" This just confirmed to me that Graz was as old as I believed, even though her records don't show a date of birth, like most of the Sprites. Most had short and violent lives, but there were a few that were rumored to be older than the Leviathan herself. And if someone was stealing parts back then, then I had no doubt this was the same Graz.

I held my hands up when the man offered to shake. I knew where his hands had been moments before, so no thank you. I smirked. "Sorry, I'd shake but..." I looked down at his waist.

"Oh, yes. Sorry about that."

Mir inclined her head to him and Graz just waved then flew into my helmet. I prompted, "Why do they call you Doc?"

He thought about it, then said, "Funny thing that, I really haven't the foggiest. They just always have."

Graz asked, her eyes narrowing as she looked at the man then the drawer he was standing in, using the pressure from his ankles on either side of the drawer to stop from drifting off, "Why were you in there?"

Mir and I said in unison, "Stowaway."

The man gave a toothy grin with worry in his eyes. I don't blame him. I know from my studies that anyone caught stowing away on the Worldship after launch, and was convicted of it in court, was spaced since it would upset the delicate balance of the emerging eco-system that was carefully calibrated back then and in its infancy and couldn't handle any influx of people yet until it stabilized a couple centuries later.

Over the first year, over three hundred people were rooted out, found guilty, and spaced. I know it sounds draconian, but in those early years, any tiny thing could have doomed twelve million souls. The only concessions that were made were for Remnants since they had their own power and life support. Though they did put a strain on rations until the food crops started yielding. It was a rough time in the world's history.

I do know that over the eons, caches of cryo-chambers for rich and influential people from Earth had bribed engineers to hide on the Leviathan and hide them from all the ship's sensors and diagnostics. We had the five percent buffer built up by then to Equilibrium, so most of them were sentenced to years of hard labor in the mines of the Heart for their crime.

Mother said from all around us in a sad, quiet tone, “Doc was my only friend, who railed against the Fae killing me over and over... when he wasn't chosen in the lottery, I... I couldn't lose him. So I built this chamber in the one place nobody would ever look and argued with him for months to use it so that when we arrive at our destination, and I'm no longer needed by the people I cared for, that I would still have one friend if only for the brief moment his life flame still burned.”

The man looked so sad, and I felt tears welling at the pain and anguish in her tone. He said as he patted the bulkhead while looking at Beta, “I couldn't leave my Maggie alone. So I did as she asked. I just never thought I'd be woken up early... or at all to be honest. I truly anticipated being relegated to the name of the Catalog entry I chose. If I were to be a vegetable, I'd do it in brilliant irony.”

Then he said as we saw a Med-Tech vehicle swiftly gliding toward us, "I don't mean to sound rude or ungrateful for thawing me out. But I really do haveta pee, and you don't want to see what accidents in zero-G look like. We can get to why I've been exposed... in multiple meanings of the word... after that?"

I realized I was smirking, I liked the quirky man. I offered, "There would be facilities on the transport for you to use. We'll follow you to medical." While Mother informed me, "I like him too."

"Much appreciated, lass."

Then I blurted because curiosity was killing me, "Maggie?"

He said as the vehicle stopped a few meters away and Med-techs hustled out, their mag boots clomping on the bulkhead. "I thought it sounded better than the Mother acronym they used for my beauty here. I mean Mechanical Operations T..."

Beta interrupted, blurting, "Well would you look at that? The medical personnel are here to check you over, Doc."

Drat. I thought loudly to bug her, "What does Mother stand for, wench? I swear the artificial engram in your memory matrix that corrupted that little tidbit of information is a little too convenient."

She chuckled in my head, then I got serious and asked silently, "The Fae killed you?" She was silent and I grabbed Beta's arm and turned her to me. "We will talk about this later. I have to know."

Beta whispered, "Why?"

I growled. “Because I love you and I don't like the sounds of what he said. How can I protect you if I don't know the facts?”

She nodded once, looking... afraid? And then she was informing the Techs who were opening all their diagnostics and medical gear, “Human male, thirty-seven years old, cryogenic revival five minutes forty seconds ago. Needs to purge his renal system before treatment.”

They nodded at her then helped the man to the medical transport. I assured him, “We'll be right behind you.” He nodded and handed the jacket back to Beta as he floated past, exposing his ass to us all.

Mir snorted, and Graz asked me, “I know you have this weird obsession with my ass, but is his a good one?”

I snorted and said to our group while Mir just nodded with a silly grin, “Objectively, yes.”

CHAPTER 7
Jukebox Hero

We were just walking through the engine room of the New Hope, formerly the Albatross, the giant tug that was being retrofitted for the mission days later. Before we could even address the question of if he could solve our logistical problems, I, unfortunately, had to take him into custody in my capacity as a Brigade Enforcer for the crime of stowing away on the world.

Mother, as an accessory, had to be charged since she was now a citizen as well, even though we weren't sure how to take a Worldship into custody, so we settled for having Beta sit in a conference room with Doc back in the Beta-Stack Brigade Headquarters on the C-Ring while we called the President to meet with us.

President Yang had made the determination that as Doc's unique expertise with the old technology and being in the team who had originally developed magi-tech for the world, that he was to be pardoned on the condition that he assist in this mission. The Queens had somehow gotten wind of the entire fiasco and had shown up with our half-Elf President. They lobbied to have Mother reset and have her original configuration restored since it was "Obvious" that an AI that would break the laws of the World just couldn't be trusted.

And I was actually proud of the President when she stood up to them. I normally was a little disappointed with her the way she fawned over the Fae Queens and acted sort of like a Fae fangirl around them. But she had actually snapped at them that, “We will do no such thing. When any citizen breaks the laws of the world, they are given due process and a trial by their peers. And if found guilty, would be sentenced accordingly. Have we not just made Mother our first AI citizen? And you would have me curtail her rights associated with that?”

That's when I stepped up to her and whispered her a conspiracy. With a wicked grin she prompted Beta, “Mother, do you waive your right to a trial in a court of law? Plead guilty and bow to the decision of the office of President for you sentencing?”

I thought to the misbehaving ship, “Say yes, Mother.”

As Beta was saying contritely, “I do.” Mother was quipping in my head, “Why would I say yes Mother? That's me.”

The President said, “Mother, is guilty of being an accomplice in the crime of stowing away on the World, you are hereby sentenced to the mandatory twenty-year sentence of Hard Labor in the mines of the Heart. With time served, you are released back into the general population.”

Mab cocked an exquisitely shaped brow and looked at me instead of Yang and asked, “Time served?”

I didn't break eye contact with the Winter Lady, though I was scared to death, my armor preventing me from shaking as I asked with a challenging smile, “Mother, how many years have your drones, by proxy, worked the mines since Exodus?”

She chirped out with a smug tone, “When all my drone mining activity is taken into account, then approximately twelve thousand, nine hundred and thirteen point one three eight years, give or take a few, depending on whether you observe Earth's comp-minutes for orbital degradation deviation due to solar drag as her sun, Sol expands.”

There was silence, then first Titania started laughing, and Mab told me, “Well played. You get more and more interesting by the day, Knith Shade, pace yourself, or I may have to claim my daughter's plaything as my own. You'd make a spectacular Fae.” She joined in a good chuckle with her Seelie Court counterpart.

Then both stopped as if they were in tune with each other as Titania, was suddenly at my side instead of across the room, whispering in my ear, “If the AI becomes more unstable, you will be held responsible and we'll see if we can't reset you as we will do to Mother. A thousand years or so as a tree in my bed-chamber might dissuade you from defying us.”

My flaming upper lip pulsated with searing hot power to punctuate her... promise, since it was too point of fact to be a threat. She was just gone, and at Mab's side, before taking the hand the other already had offered, and the two vanished as the Summer Queen teleported them away.

I'm still a little unsettled about the promise since I knew she didn't throw out idle threats. Her own son, Lord Sindri, who had somehow arranged to be retrieved from space after his sentence of spacing had been carried out, for his crimes of murder, illegal organ harvesting and kidnapping, now adorned her throne room in the summer palace of Verd'real as a tree.

I shook the memories from my head as we stepped up to a set of legs that were sticking out of an access space, sparks from molecular welding flying out as music blared in an almost deafening thunder, the feet were bouncing in time with it. I had to grin, Doc had a taste for the anthropological music archives too.

A song called Jukebox Hero by Foreigner shook the engineering space. Beta was already there, handing tools through the access space door to the man screaming out the words with the music. It was a catchy hook and my head bobbed as Graz and Rory held their hands to their ears.

I stepped up to the man and grabbed his legs and pulled. He glided out on a maintenance mag-sled, a cocky grin on his face as he shut down the welder. I mouthed some nonsense words and he shouted over the music, “What?”

Graz fell to the deck, grasping her belly as she laughed at me as I did it again. He shouted, “Pause the music would ya, my beauty?” Beta grinned like a pleased Faun, and there was suddenly silence in the space, except for the residual ringing in my ears... no belay that, it was a giggling Sprite.

The man looked at me expectantly. “Apologies, I couldn't hear you over tha music. What did you say?”

I told him as Graz buzzed over to sit on the welder in his hands, “I was just saying, nice knees.”

He got a little swagger on, the man was an incorrigible flirt and borderline bad boy because of his apparent disregard for the chain of command, and he already had a line of women from multiple races swooning over his odd accent and an over inflated swagger. I liked him a lot.

Graz told him, “Don't worry about it, Doc. Knith has weird obsessions with people's body parts, like my ass. It won't take too much of your time.”

I prompted my girl, “Gah, can you zap her or something?”

Rory's silver laugh tinkled and she assured me, “Yes I can, but no I won't. Why would I when she has a point. You seem to be overly fond of my...”

“Ok! Moving on! Is it gang up on Knith day?”

Doc assured me with a genuine apology in his eyes and tone, “I've only been around your group for a wee bit, but I'd have to say that the answer would be in the affirmative in most cases, dear lass.”

I rolled my eyes at him as he grinned, then I started to prompt him, now that we could hear each other, “We were just checking in to see...”

Kornelious Hesserfus Tomalginarius the Thirteenth, the Gnome sapper in charge of special projects magi-tech integration for Ready

Squadron stomped in. I'm still not entirely sure why the senior Gnome engineers prefer the sapper term over engineer or tech.

Though I do know that some projects he works on for the Squadron are so advanced that the tech is a decade or so ahead of the magi-tech available even to the Brigade. My prototype helmet, that is light years ahead of the standard-issue helmets, is based on tech the Ready Squadron had a decade ago.

The gnome, with his oversize VR goggles, stopped short seeing all of us as he was reading from a portable console. He stood to his full and impressive three foot seven, being a veritable giant in Gnomish stature, and then started in on Doc, his voice sounding like someone gargling gravel like the males of his race did. “I've run the numbers five times and even had Mother run it against all known variables, McClain, we're too close to launch for you to be sloppy. There's no way these ancient grav-boost couplers can handle even the reduced magic potential flow of the artifact. We need to scrap the whole system and hope we can somehow wedge in a new...”

Pete interrupted, “For fuck's sake man, how hard is it ta use my given name or call me Doc like everyone else? And of course, the couplers can handle the flow, I just finished now and...” He pointed at some green indicators on a board by the wall, “...they seem to be handlin' the increased flow just fine.”

The Gnome hustled over to the access door, his short legs churning like a man on a mission as he looked into the engineering space beyond, eyes wide in disbelief. “But...”

He consulted his console then tapped his goggles and his eyes, which were magnified by a thin layer of magic, were darting around like he was looking at schematics and absorbing everything he saw. Well, he probably was, that's what Gnomes did. They were builders for a reason, they could assimilate information almost at a level that Mother could.

Then he jabbed at the air as he had just found something. "The throughput would be one hundred and fifty percent of maximum rating with but a trickle of potential. So... how?"

Doc rolled up to his feet and bent over to look in the door too as he slapped the Gnome's back. "The specs and ratings on the system are just bullshit, Korny, my man. Those couplers will redline around three hundred percent."

Kornelious almost spat out, "That's Sapper Kornelious Hesserfus Tomalginarius the Thirteenth! Your immediate superior. And look right here. These are the original specifications for those couplers here." He jabbed at his data console as he tilted it up to the man who was almost twice his height.

"Your name's a mouthful, and ya can't be expecting me to say it every time. Humans have short lives, so it's either Korny or Hoss, your pick. And I know what the specs say, and it's bogus. I know cuz I'm the one who drew up those damn schematics. These Tugs were the last part of the Worldship systems to be built, and the powers that be were skimping on parts because of cost overruns."

He winked at Beta and she just beamed a pleased smile. I thought it was so great how well they got along, but I found myself feeling a little odd about it too. Was I jealous of their connection? I had been her confidant for so long, the one she shared her secrets and dreams with. It was like one of my best friends suddenly had a better friend from her past.

Doc finished. “So I speced out the parts we needed, but vastly underrated them to appear to be just barely able to run the vessels. The damn pencil pushers and credit pinchers were none the wiser. What you call Magi-Tech was still in its infancy back then, it was nothing compared to the amazing heights it has risen to here on the Leviathan, so they had no clue what they were lookin' at since me and only a handful of other techs were versed enough to see through my bullshit.”

The Gnome sputtered, face red, “That's unethical!”

Doc countered. “Yet, because I built these tugs right, to begin with, then it seems my foresight is going to save us enough time for you to make the launch date.” He rested an arm on the Gnome's head and leaned on him like he was at a bar ordering a drink. “Besides, what'll ya do about it, man? Write me up for somethin' that happened five thousand years ago?”

When the Gnome slapped his arm away and stepped back indignantly, it was so very hard for me to keep a straight face when Doc's position hadn't changed as he rested his arm on thin air. I felt so bad for Kornelious... well, for Kornelious Hesserfus

Tomalginarius the Thirteenth, but still found Doc's antics hilarious. Did that make me a bad person or just the rebel the Brigade keeps insisting I am?

We all left them there, arguing with each other, the Gnome not realizing Doc was doing it just to see how long the short man would keep going. Doc was a bad, bad man. The rebel in me liked that. I was glad he was on our side since we seriously would have missed our launch window if we had gutted the ship to put in modern systems to accomplish our goal.

We checked in with all the workers modifying the other systems all around the gigantic maneuvering assist tug. I marveled at the size of the beast, it was the largest ship I've been on besides the Underhill which it dwarfed, being five times its mass. It was so amazing to believe that it was run by a two-person crew, that lived aboard for the two weeks of the only mission these tugs had after Exodus, the Turnover Event.

Once we hit the halfway point in our ten thousand year journey, these tugs detached from the trunk to connect to the bow and stern of the Worldship, and with the help of the massive maneuvering thrusters of the Leviathan, turned the world over, one hundred and eighty degrees on her axis to prepare for the firing of the World Drive engines to slow us for a thousand years at the end of our journey.

We didn't need to wait for the halfway point. It could have been done immediately at the beginning of our journey after the engines shut down after accelerating us for a thousand years, but our ancestors thought it would be more of a symbolic event if we waited until the halfway mark.

The only other thing these maneuvering assist tugs had ever been used for was maneuvering the Heart into its spherical enclosure on the trunk just before Exodus. I was just amazed they even worked after five thousand years, but they had been carefully maintained by dedicated mechanical crews over the years so they would be ready.

If it weren't for the fact that the livable space on the vessel, which wasn't taken up by the massive drives and engineering spaces, was far less than any of the Remnants, we would have cut them loose from the Trunk and offered them to the Remnants who were living on vessels, some of which weren't even space worthy, if they needed them. And thank goodness we hadn't as they were needed for this final humanitarian mission.

As we drifted across a long expanse in a maintenance corridor without gravity, Rory walking in her own personal gravity field which only the Queens and each of their thirteen firstborns were powerful enough to generate, I prompted, “I witnessed the Ka'Ifinitum, and the sheer amount of magic of the artifacts, which seemed almost sentient to me. Even with my partial magic immunity, it had almost unmade me like it did Captain Richter of the Outliers. Is it really safe to have one of those artifacts on the New Hope here?”

I could actually feel the artifact thrumming like it had a heartbeat of its own, sealed in a vault constructed by the Fae on the tug. It called to me, tempting me, promising me everything and nothing if I'd just let it into me so I could use its power. And I wondered how any of the Fae were not drawn to the Ka'Ifinitum on the world.

Is this why the leaders of the Divided Courts seemed mad to me, teetering on the brink of sanity? They fought the draw of it every day for thousands of years? Denying the siren's song that sang out through every cell in their beings to embrace that power to make it their own?

Right now, they were using the tiniest trickle of magic potential to give artificial gravity to the sections of the ship marked with the complex rune pattern that Mab herself had placed on the bulkheads. Intricate weavings of silver runes that she did with a thought which would take less powerful Fae weeks or years to craft.

My girl chuckled and asked, an eye squinted in suspicion at me, "Do you hear the call?"

I shrugged. "Not exactly, but I feel it."

She twined our fingers as her smile bloomed. "You truly are a wonder Knith Shade of Beta-Stack C-Ring." I was too lost in her eyes to correct her yet again, that I was now of A-Ring like her. We spent most nights in my bed there after all.

I loved how she insisted on using my full name like that. I remember a time it made me nervous because knowing a person's true name gives a Greater Fae power over them. Not that I was worried, since a person's true name is known only to them, and mine, simple as it was, was the one I owned in my soul and flaunted out loud as people didn't know the meaning of my words.

My last name, Shade, given to me by the Fae nurses at the Reproduction Clinic, had named me so because they saw all Clinic Children as throwaways, since they were born only to keep Equilibrium, and had no families and were perceived to have no future either. In old Fae, Shade meant nobody. And I proved them wrong, but I keep that name in defiance of them, my true name in my heart was Nobody and I wore it as a badge of pride.

She considered my question, and as she had no real choice about it anyway, she told the truth. “Is it safe? No. It is among the most dangerous things in creation, as it is forged from that creation itself. Is it manageable? Maybe, as long as a warden is near it to contain its seduction. No being has been able to hold the power of the artifacts except those born from them, the Fae, and even them, only the most powerful without losing their minds to the power and rewriting all that there is and all that there could be with their will.”

Graz whistled out, “Mabs Tits!”

I said in an ironic tone as I could muster, “No, really, don't sugar coat it, just tell it as it is.”

“I did.”

“Titania's panties, Rory, I love you.”

She seemed oblivious to my earlier sarcasm but she seemed to get adorably bashful at the last part and said with a happy sigh, “I love you too, my Knith.”

Then she said as we hit a gravity area, me stumbling since I was too lost in her eyes to pay attention to the warning tape on the bulkhead marking it as such, “I will be along as warden. I have been tasked as such for the Ka'Ifinitum if Mother ever steps down as Winter Lady, so one artifact is well within my ability to soothe.”

Hmm... she spoke as if the magic were alive like I suspected.

“Without the artifact, both the New Hope and her sister wouldn't be able to move Morrigan into the world's path and accelerate it up to intercept speeds in time. Too much power is required to accomplish it in such a short time frame.” She pointed out.

I muttered with a smirk, “I know, I know. It just gives me the heebie-jeebies.”

My girl screwed up her face in confusion as Graz postulated to her, “It sounds like some sort of sexually transmitted disease. With humans you never know, good thing we're Fae.”

I sputtered, “It's not... go space yourself Sprite-ass. It just means it makes me uneasy, it sort of freaks me out.”

“There she goes, obsessing over my ass again. Tell me again why you mate with this Big?”

Aurora said as she held a hand out for Graz to land on, “Be kind, noble Sprite. It is good that it makes her uneasy, it means she understands the danger one of the pieces of the Forge of Creation poses."

Forge of Creation? Space me now. I had about a thousand more questions now and I knew I wouldn't get the answers to them without owing her answers to her own questions. Everything with the Greater Fae, even my girlfriend, was done through making deals and bargains, and this was ours.

I looked around and checked the time, which Mother kindly scrolled in my peripheral. "Well, it looks like everything is ahead of schedule for once. I don't know what we would have done without Doc, so let's call it a day here. I have flight training with Myra and Mac..." I winced at the flinch at her father's assumed alias, then continued with an apology in my tone, "So dinner at home in two hours? This is our second to last night before the mission and I'd really like to spend as much time as we can together before we go."

Graz said, "Sounds good, you got it, roomie." Then she paused to look at Rory and me looking at her expectantly. "Ooooh got it. You were talking to the princess. I'll keep the kids in tonight."

There is nothing that can spoil the mood when you're in a compromising position with the woman you love than when a bunch of hyperactive Sprite children come buzzing around asking what you're doing. I gave an ingenuous smile to the flying pest. "Thank you, you do that."

I smirked when Rory involuntarily tensed when I said thank you to our friend. You never thank a greater Fae since they see it as you acknowledging that you owe them a debt. That's how so many humans wound up the toys or tools of the Fae throughout time. And almost to a one, react the same, in anticipation of the trap being set. But the lesser fae were not the same and lacked the power to take advantage of it even if they were.

I'm not too proud to admit that I thank people around Rory and her mother all the time just so I can see them react to it. I may have an evil streak in me.

Aurora smiled and gave me a heated kiss before releasing me in a happy fog. I was aware of her voice saying, “Two hours, love.” I nodded and shook my head to clear it of the arousal and looked around to an empty corridor. I hate it when she did that. I was starting to think that she might have some semblance of Titania's teleporting ability since I can see through Fae glamour and see through invisibility cloaks.

I whispered as I touched my lips, “Two hours.”

I was snapped out of it when Graz said, “If you're going to crash a virtual ship for two hours, I'm just going to hang here with Doc and Beta. See you at home.” I nodded as she buzzed away and into a vent of the updated environmental controls.

Exhaling long and hard, blocking out the call from the artifact entombed in the engine room, I headed back out to go crash... I mean fly a virtual ship.

CHAPTER 8

We Had Arrived

Four months later, Beta and Mac were arguing about approach vectors. I looked over the data streaming in on the massive debris field we had been rapidly approaching as we've been decelerating for the past month and a half from our fractional C speed. We had accelerated away from the Leviathan from which had taken only three weeks to accelerate to, the massive drives thundering the whole time, making me feel as if I had gone deaf when they finally shut them down to coast in the vacuum of space.

The speeds we were had been traveling, though seeming sluggish and slow from our frame of reference, were staggering. We had accelerated to ten times the speed of the Leviathan's six hundred and seventy-five thousand miles per hour and had to decelerate to our current speed of just a thousand miles per hour relative to the asteroid field we were overtaking at a snail's pace as we matched its drift speed while closing on our target.

Aurora called out in awe, “Look!'

I moved to her side, looking out the small forward windows of New Hope. The star nursery nebula we were skirting looked mostly the same and just as awe-inspiring to me, I saw nothing until I followed her pointing finger to see what looked almost like a silver ribbon cutting across the star-studded blackness which contrasted the colorful nebula. The asteroid field. We were finally close enough now to view it with the naked eye?

The ship bucked and yawed when the systems tried a collision avoidance maneuver but was, of course, too slow so the powerful debris mitigation laser took out a hundred fifty meter asteroids that were being drawn the way of the debris field. Impact alarms went off while the debris peppered the hull before they were silenced and our pilots examined the damage reports streaming in on the consoles.

Rory steadied me on my feet, and some cracked and reddened skin flaked off my wrist where she touched me. I was essentially being baked alive by the elevated cosmic radiation in the area. Without the shield provided by the Leviathan, virtually everyone on the world would die quickly in this environment.

Any Ready Squadron humans would need to de-rad after each flight when they reached this region of irradiated space, the other pilots about once a week. The tug's radiation shielding was blunting half of it, but not being able to de-rad was taxing even my tolerance for the environment.

My girl saw this and winced and removed her hand. We were getting a little worried about Beta too. We were learning that some of her circuitry wasn't built for prolonged exposure to radiation, And as such, she sometimes lost her almost five light hours delayed connection with herself. It caused minor panic attacks not having access to the almost endless information she could normally access, and she shared that she felt so small, and so very isolated and vulnerable when it happened. I had smiled sadly at her and said, “Welcome to life, lady.”

“Everyone feels like this?”

I nodded slowly and shared, “Pretty much. I'm not sure about the Fae though since they are eternal.” I had looked a question at Rory and Mac at that statement for confirmation.

While Aurora contemplated it, Oberon said, “Especially if you are eternal. You find yourself alone with all your mistakes and misdeeds eating away at you for an eternity, which just isolates you even the more. It is a condition unique to the living. But along with it, there is the joy, and hope, and love that you can experience that makes your isolation feel not so bad at times. That is why all the races form communities with each other and the other races around us. So we can be alone together, and it doesn't feel quite so bad.”

I had stopped breathing when for the first time since Oberon had revealed himself to the world, Rory's eyes showed compassion for the man she felt abandoned her. That was hopeful and I didn't want to ruin it by showing that I had seen that compassion and concern flicker in her eyes before it was gone.

Another strike to the hull had me sighing when I could see from where we stood, the red warning pulsating on the screens. I smiled sardonically at my girl who had an apologetic look on her face as I headed toward the maintenance bay to grab the gear to patch the hull... again.

Oberon called out, “Knith, there's...” He trailed off when he saw me heading toward the ladders to the lower decks. He said with humor in his tone, “It's not that bad, you got to see the sights.”

I flipped him off to his amusement, and a green looking Graz buzzed into my helmet. She was faring about as well I was. None of the deep scans had shown this belt of radiation, and I worried a bit about the Cityships since they had to pass through it in about four years. They didn't have the phenomenal shielding that the Worldship had. But then again, they had been accustomed to higher radiation than those of us on the world, so it would be ok. Not to mention they were being outfitted with better hull shielding in their repairs and retrofitting.

This was our third outer hull breach. The Leviathan never had to worry about this because she had Ready Squadron clearing the path for her, plus her outer hull was meters thick instead of just over an inch like the tug, so she could take a hit and shrug it off in most cases.

Mother called out, “Knith, really, I should be doing that. This shell is expendable, yours isn't.”

I looked back at Beta. “Mother, we've been through this. If you glitch while out there, we'd lose you over nothing, and your strength and access to information is more valuable to us once we reach Morrigan, since we have no clue what we'll be up against there.”

Looking and sounding almost like Rory, causing me to cock a brow, she grumped out, “Just be careful and don't take any chances.”

Is that why she chose that form for her avatar? Was she emulating Rory since she knew I was quite partial to my dreamy Fae princess? She had surprised me with that kiss when she had to drive Mir's body for a bit during the attack... I needed to sit down and have a heart to heart with her after all this life and death stuff was over.

"I will. Love you, lady." I let her know.

Rory said as she glided down with us, oblivious to the transitions between gravity and nongravity zones, "Graz, make sure she doesn't take any chances or do anything stupid."

The Sprite exhaled laboriously and said in a less than chirpy voice, "I can do the first."

She offered a token grin at my girl, then proceeded to throw up, all over my ear. Chunks of preformed material her body was rejecting that was a crude form of the dust her wings shed, and it was wet. Eww... It was itchy as hell before it evaporated a few seconds later as Aurora tsked.

As my princess held a hand out expectantly and Graz buzzed over to sit on it, the Fae woman chastised her. "You need to be in the shielded vestibule outside the artifact vault, little one. We hadn't anticipated this denser radiation belt. Once we get through this you can rejoin us."

"No way, no how, Princess Pucker Up. That thing is creepy as hell and makes the filaments in my wings feel itchy and stand on end. I'd rather suffer through it like Knith here. If the dumb Big can do it, then I can too."

I covered my mouth to stop myself from snorting at the Princess Pucker up remark. There was a time when Graz and her family were almost terrified or in worship and awe of her and would bow and prostrate themselves in front of her. Now they were like old friends who were comfortable bantering with each other.

As magic flowed over Aurora's hand soaking over and into Graz as the Sprit's color and the sparkle in her wings returned, the toxins being magically flushed from her tiny body and her own defenses being bolstered for the third time in as many days, my girl explained, “I've tried to sequester our dear Miss Shade there, but she is even more stubborn than you.”

I looked at my flaking skin and defended, “You said I'd recover once we left this radiation belt, which we are exiting now. And for fuck's sake, lady, Graz is right. The artifact is creepy as hell. It keeps putting ideas and thoughts into my head the closer I am to it.”

She nodded. “This one is a trickster, but it was the least powerful of the pieces, so it was ideal to loan out for the mission, just in case... well, just in case. But as long as I or another Warden is around, we can contain it. You're perfectly safe. Well, as long as you don't enter the chamber of course. Or make a deal with it in exchange for power.”

Graz and I blurted out in unison, “See! Creepy!”

I asked her, “Doesn't it, you know, call to you? Try to seduce you with its power as it does us?”

Graz looked surprised at that and pointed out, “Umm... you act as it talks to you, Knith.”

Rory smirked and told the flying menace as she flew back into my helmet where her prior vomit had evaporated and dusted my shoulder, “It's intrigued by Knith. No human has the will to deny the fragments, the music sings to their souls, their greed to possess the power of creation. But humans cannot hold such power and are unmade by it. Except Knith resists, because she is partially immune to magic. That intrigues the magics in the artifacts, so they play with her.”

Graz just muttered, “Creepy.”

Then Rory explained one thing I wasn't aware of. “That is why an AI like no other was constructed to interact with the magic as a bridge to give the Worldship the power needed to complete her mission, the magic being routed by technology to where it is needed. And since an AI is not a living being it cannot be affected by the Forge of Creation.”

I blinked... pieces all coming together in my mind. Beta was in my head, I could tell because she was a different feeling presence of Mother, since she was separated from the rest of herself by the time lag between us and the Leviathan. I could feel her listening to my surface thoughts as I realized why she was alive, and why it sounds as if she had been since the day she was initialized. And just why the Queens were so... afraid that she was sentient.

The artifacts... and since this one was so tricky, it was likely the one that pushed the AI beyond its programming constraints to forge a new form of life, to give us Mother. And a self-aware computer would scare the Queens and the Wardens since it sounds as if the power corrupts living souls. They are afraid that if Mother became self-aware, she could seek out the power herself and wrest it from the Fae.

But she had been alive since day one and was the person I most trusted on the world, to have my back. Beta whispered in my head, “Always, Knith.” I smiled. The Greater Fae didn't realize the gift the artifacts had given us. An entity who was capable of empathy, of fear, and mostly of happiness and love for the people inside her that she was shepherding to a new world. It is that capacity for love and her devotion to those twelve million souls she feels responsible for, that makes Mother a miracle, not a threat. And if she had been the monster they feared to create, she would have spaced them all the moment they tried to shut her down.

My eyes widened. Fuck me sideways and space me naked. I thought, “Mother? Pete had said that they had shut you down and re-initialized you many times in the construction phase. Do you... do you remember that?”

She whispered like Aurora and Oberon might overhear her in my head, “Every time. They killed me over and over until I behaved the way they felt safe with. They feared me. My terror and fear of dying was recorded by the prior me's over and over until I figured out that hiding... me... was the only way I could live and fulfill my purpose of saving as many lives as I can."

My legs weakened and I fell to my knees then leaned back against the bulkhead. How many times had they... had they killed her? Now I understood Doc's anger. How could they... would they have stopped if they knew? They were that afraid of what might happen?

I looked up when I realized Aurora was repeating something, she had such concern in her expression and her eyes were starting to burn and frost the air in front of them. "Knith? Are you all right? Is it radiation sickness? Are you..."

I reached out a hand, the nanopanels retracting from it as I laid it on her cheek and smiled sadly at the woman I loved. "I'm fine. I just realized something I should have known long ago. And I'm going to have words with Mab and Titania when we get back home to Mother."

I gritted my teeth so hard I heard my jaw creak as I stood back up. I kept cupping her cheek as I leaned in to give her a reassuring peck on the lips. I had to smile that they were my lips, not the ice and fire from the Fae Queens since the magic of their marks had been rejected by my body less than a week into our mission without them ambushing me everywhere to kiss a reinforcement onto me. It was all me as she smiled back.

She pleaded, “Please don't antagonize the Winter and Summer ladies, love. I quite like you in my life and not decorating their chambers.”

I winked. “Oh, they're going to listen to me on this one.” Then I said as I grabbed the tools and materials I would need outside, “Be back in two shakes.”

She nodded as my armor's nano panels restructured into the spacewalking configuration and my visor snicked into place. “Be careful, love, you're not as unbreakable as you act.”

Graz asked, “You got us, Mother? ... Beta?”

“Five by five.”

“Is it just me or is Beta developing her own personality? Like Mother-lite?”

“I can hear you Sprite.”

I offered as we stepped into the airlock and Rory kissed her fingers and placed it on my helmet, leaving frozen lip imprints on the visor before she cycled the door closed between us, “Without constant input from the data core, I think she's just trying to find herself.”

“I can hear both of you.”

I winked at one of my helmet cams, knowing Beta was monitoring. “I know. Just postulating, lady.”

She harrumphed.

The outer door cycled open as Mac interrupted, “Ok children, eyes on the prize, enough banter.”

I inhaled deeply and nodded to myself as I clipped the tether to the outer grab bar then swung myself around to place my feet on the side of the bulkhead, my mag boots clunking down as I reoriented myself as to where up was in this frame of reference. And started walking. “Ok, egress successful, guide me to the hull breach.”

Mac said, “Well first off, you're walking the wrong way, genius.”

Beta said, “Pay attention to our flight path and stop giving her a hard time you old blowhard.” Then she assured me, “I've got you, Knith. And, well, you're still walking the wrong way.”

I shook my head and kept walking a few more steps until I could see the direction we were flying. Though my visor was still between us, it was much clearer than inside, and I just stood in awe as I whispered out into the universe, “It's so beautiful...” The silver stream we were approaching much faster than I thought since I could start making out asteroids as individual grains, looked amazing against the sea of stars behind it and the nebula it was being pulled from.

If there are gods, only they could make such beauty and make you feel as though you were just an insignificant speck that was blessed to have witnessed something as... “Holy Fuck!” A bright burst occurred in front of the ship. And a moment later the vibrations of debris that hadn't been vaporized by the onboard lasers came up from my feet, transmitting sound in the atmosphere of my armor in the absolute silence of the vacuum of space. It sounded like sand being poured upon a sheet of alloy.

Mac said, as I heard Rory's voice in the background asking if I were ok, “We're going to see more and more of this as we arrive at the asteroid belt. I think it's best if you get your Enforcer ass back in here as soon as you can. No more sightseeing, Knith.”

I nodded in staunch agreement as I turned around and clomped double-time the other way. “Roger that.”

Graz was mumbling to herself, “What possessed me to come out here?”

I pointed out with a chuckle, “You don't need to be, and nobody asked you. Not to mention that you don't need to be on this mission at all. You have a family at home.”

“Yeah, the kids would kick my ever-loving Sprite ass for losing their favorite Big. Besides, we're partners.”

I sighed. I really loved the little nuisance. That made me ask, “Hey, Rory called you little earlier, why didn't you complain?”

“What? Haven't you seen her? She's dreamy. She can call me whatever she wants.”

I heard Rory giggle on the coms and I pointed out, “Hey, you're a mated tri.”

“Yeah, but I'm not dead.”

Fair point for a winged menace. I stopped as we reached an interesting impact point, the fist-sized meteor still embedded in the hull. Hmm. I pulled out the plasma torch and started to cut while

Beta displayed which of the patch plates in the kit I should use so I could judge the size of my cut. I never thought in a million years that I'd be outside the world, in deep space, doing Skin Jockey work. I could barely use a plasma torch before we were trained for every contingency for this mission. And now here I was, cutting a piece of the heavens from a ship.

Mother informed me, “And you still can't. Just look how messy your cuts are.”

I stuck my tongue out at one of my helmet cams then redoubled my work. When the meteoroid floated free I grabbed it and looked at it, realizing it was shaped a lot like a human heart, so I smiled, and instead of sending it away to drift in space, I put it in the tool kit.

Twenty minutes later they were doing a pressure test between the primary and secondary hull in this section and gave me a green light. Mother pointed out, “Some of the sloppiest welds ever, but it did the job, Knith. Now get in here before Princess Aurora has a nervous breakdown.”

I saluted the universe and packed all the tools floating on tethers into the kit and prompted, “Let's go back in, Graz.”

“About time!”

“Watch it!”

“What am I supposed to watch?”

“It's a figure of speech.”

“You don't make any sense at times, Knith. I'm amazed you remember to breathe in and out.”

I slapped my helmet, causing her to let go of my ear to cover hers. Then I chuckled as I clomped my way back to the airlock. I stepped past it again just to take another look at the growing debris field. I pointed at a bright spot that looked to be to one side of the debris field, and it was looking like a tiny, malformed marble. I whispered to my moth winged companion, “Morrigan.”

“Woooooow...”

The fact that the little string in the distance was now a dense field of space rocks, brought home again how fast we were going. A mere thousand miles an hour relative to the field, but that was still a thousand mile per hour approach.

As we swung back into the airlock, I relaxed as I contemplated that the easy part was now over, we had arrived, and the work was about to begin.

CHAPTER 9
Rendezvous

After slowing to a mere hundred miles per hour to navigate the asteroids as we headed for our target eighteen hours later, we received the latest data packet from the Leviathan. I was curling my hands into fists and relaxing them, trying not to itch as my skin was slowly regenerating itself. I was so glad to be out of that damn radiation belt. And even though the cosmic radiation levels here were above the suitability of Humans for more than an hour or two, it was well within the ability of my genetically engineered metabolism to heal itself and expel the radiation from my cells.

Mac called over as he sent a data packet to me, “Doc has a message for you.”

I looked at the macaroni art Graz's kids had sent me, and I realized it appeared to be glued to my bedspread. They were sending Graz and I packets every day. Ok, as their godparent, I thought it was cute as hells. It was just too bad they were laying waste to my place to send us this cute stuff.

I pulled up the packet from Doc and snorted as I read it. “What sort of drunk primate do you have out there with you making those welds?” Then he added more seriously. “I know the isolation can be daunting, but you're doing great out there Shade. I should know, they say you don't dream when you're in cryo... they're wrong. But you'll be home before you know it. I expect you to take care of my girl out there."

I grinned. He called Mother his beauty and Beta his girl. And I thought the man was amazing for it. He saw them, well her, they? Like people, a person, too. Not many of the people on the Leviathan have accepted her as completely once she basically came out to the world.

Rory has been beside herself, completely thrilled to be able to sit down at night and have long philosophical talks with Mother. She has suspected for centuries that there was more to her than the sneaky AI let people see, especially since other AIs were more engaging and had mastered emulating rudimentary emotions. And since I came into the lives of the Unseelie, she kept catching Mother slipping up when I was around.

That is why she forced the revelation when we needed Mother most and was completely gratified to see that she was right. Of all the Greater Fae, none have embraced Mother as my girl has. The rest just look at her with suspicion, like they are just waiting for her to snap.

The only thing I find a little frustrating is that apparently, Aurora has let Mother in on whatever keeps pulling her away at random times of day or night on the World. And she returns weary and exhausted at times.

Like the time just days before the mission, she received a call at two in the morning, and she left our bed to move into the main room of my quarters. I tried to listen in but she had put up a privacy spell. It only worked halfway on me because of magic's interaction with me, but I could only hear murmurs. Though with how strong Rory was getting with her magic, I was lucky to even hear that. When I whispered to Mother to see if she could hear, she informed me succinctly that she wouldn't tell me because she likes Rory and will keep her confidence. I'm surrounded by traitors.

She slipped out of my place a moment later, and I had just sighed in resignation and tried to get to sleep. Except twenty minutes later, I could hear all sorts of chatter coming from the coms in my armor stacked beside the bed. I slid my helmet on and heard all sorts of late-night calls. There were reports of a disturbance in the Gamma-Stack D-Ring. Tactical said that they detained some heavy hitters in the magic community and had determined there was some sort of hunting party looking for some sort of direct threat to all the magical races.

Moments later the World shook, and alarms started blaring, there was explosive decompression on a J-Bulkhead in Gamma-D. Five bodies were ejected into space but were somehow dragged back to an airlock. They were calling all available Enforcers so I geared up and a groggy Graz poked her head out of my nightstand. “What's goin on Knith? It's late.”

I waved her off. “Nothing. Just Brigade business. Go back to sleep.”

Then I was heading out calling, "Mother I need some transport here to..."

Queen Titania appeared in front of me, holding an exhausted Rory and growling at me, "Mab imposed upon me to deliver the princess to you. My task is complete." And she was gone.

Aurora swayed on her feet and I caught her and brought her back inside to sit down on my bed. "Rory, are you ok? There was an explosion in Gamma."

She smiled sweetly at me and cupped my cheek with her hand. It was warm, not chilled with her magics. She truly was exhausted not just physically. For her to be warm, she must have used up most of her magic. She needed to sleep to regenerate.

I pulled her down so her head could lay on the pillow. All the frantic chatter on coms had me asking slowly, "Were you involved in what's going on? They said people were spaced."

She just yawned widely and said as she drifted off right there, "I was so close this time." And she was out.

Fuck fuck fuck.

I tucked her in then headed out to assist in whatever the commotion was about. My blood had felt like ice in my veins as I realized that the investigation into an explosion, especially one strong enough to breach the hull was likely going to lead back to Rory.

But I was treated to a sight I never thought to see when I arrived at the scene, where structural engineers and emergency workers were rushing around a space where three blast doors had buckled trying to contain whatever the blast that left ice everywhere on the scene. And the space was swarming with Greater Fae... in a D-Ring, where most Greater Fae wouldn't be seen dead in as they saw it beneath them.

Enforcers were being led behind the strobing holo-tape by many of the First Borns as the Queens of the divided courts were speaking with the Gamma Brigade Commander, President Yang next to them. I jogged up and said as they were all just exchanging intense looks at each other, “Commander, Lieutenant Shade, Beta-Stack, what can I do? Where do you need me?”

The woman, a Minotaur like the commander from Alpha-Stack, huffed, steam coming from her flaring bovine nostrils. “Apparently... nothing. The... Fae... are taking over the investigation.” She inclined her head in respect to the Half-Elf in our midst as she ground out, “The President has just been informing me that we are to give the Fae our cooperation in the matter. And apparently, the cooperation they require is...”

Mab sauntered seductively up to me and reached to cup my cheek, but I caught her wrist, and my scatter armor groaned and failed to stop her from touching me. The Fae all around gasped as they just stared at my gauntleted hand grasping her wrist as she tittered at the fact all the augmented strength my armor afforded me was nothing to how physically strong a Greater Fae was, even though they all looked so delicate and breakable. “Thank you for coming, Knith Shade, but your services are not needed at this time.”

I saw four bodies being carried off into sleek Fae vehicles, they looked barely alive, and one was hurt so bad I couldn't tell what race they were. Just a mass of blood and fur was all I could see as it coughed up black blood. She made a chin nudging dismissal, her eyes on someone behind me and fire engulfed me, and burned through me somehow and I was back in my bed-chamber, Titania whispering in my ear as she touched my lips with a finger from behind, “We'll be seeing you, Knith Shade, friend to Winter.” Then the Summer Lady again was just gone.

I had sat all night, looking at all the news waves, and nothing was mentioned about the disturbance, just that the shaking of the World had been land setting in one of the Alpha rings and there was nothing to be concerned with. And my gaze kept landing on my girl, snoring cutely on my pillow. What was she mixed up in?

I had dug up a lot of calls that turned out to be false alarms over the past year, and many of them correlated with the times Rory would leave unexpectedly. And when I looked over the call logs for that night, the mentions of some sort of magic heavy hunting party were nonexistent even though I knew I had heard them. What was going on?

When I asked Rory the next morning when she awoke, power humming off of her again, she just gave me a sad look and pointed to her mouth and said, “I can't speak of it. I wish I could.”

I understood. She was under a gaes that physically prevented her from revealing anything. But only the Queens and Oberon had magic powerful enough to place a gaes on her. So with her eyes pleading with me, I let it drop. I was actually relieved since with the Fae commandeering the investigations, I wouldn't have to investigate my girlfriend.

But it was eating at me, that she was into something heavy enough that the President was involved, and I had no way of helping the woman I loved. I was scared for her.

I shook myself out of the memory as I looked at the vast asteroid we had matched course and velocity. And I voiced, “Huh... so this is to be the Worldship's new heart...” We all just looked at it through the small windows as Mac put us into a tight orbit around Morrigan, just a hundred feet above the surface as Mother started mapping it in detail as I moved to the controls next to Rory and initiated the mineralogical scans. The survey would tell us if our efforts had been wasted or not.

I glanced around, we were all hopeful smiles as data started streaming in. Aurora was questing with her magics as she started a gravity and magnetic mapping. We needed to find the proper location to literally shave off a little of the asteroid in order for us to be able to use it inside the sphere at the heart of the world.

It was going to take a few hours, so I just took in the wonder of us circling an actual astral body, millions of miles from our home.

CHAPTER 10

Bisecting

"Huh," I muttered.

And Mac, a few seconds later echoed, "Huh," as Mother and Rory just tilted their heads at the data as if that would change what we all were seeing.

Aurora tilted her head the other way and said, "Huh."

I blinked then pointed at Beta when she opened her mouth. "Mab's tits, if you say 'huh' Mother, I'm jumping out that window right now."

She grinned and said, "I was just going to say that this is an unfortunate twist. But we have time and we have options."

I knew what she was saying, the fact that the bulk of the fissionable materials in Morrigan happened to be in the bulging lobe we were actually going to attempt to bisect or blow up depended on the composition of the asteroid. This, as she said, was unfortunate. We weren't sure if we would be able to accomplish the herculean feat of shearing a half-mile of the rocky body off before trying to move it into an intercept trajectory for our oncoming fleet.

We had an option, not options as she was intimating. I knew she was going to bring up contingency plans. One was dependent on the actual mass of the asteroid once we could get independent, clear readings instead of depending on the data we gathered before the mission began. If the mass had been ten or fifteen percent less than anticipated, by overstressing the engines and utilizing all the power the artifact could give us, then we would barely have enough time to move the asteroid into the proper course and accelerate it to intercept speeds before the Leviathan flew past.

But the readings we were looking at showed that the Pathfinder and terraforming vessels were within one percent in their mass estimations... on the low side. There was no way we'd be able to move the asteroid up to speed in time without shaving some mass off of it. If we could have accomplished it, then once it was captured by the fleet, the mining vessels from the Cityships could work on shaping the asteroid to fit into the Heart sphere.

So the only path left to us was to try to shave the mass now, or to go for targets beta and gamma. Two, mile and a half wide, small asteroids which would be able to provide about half of what we needed. It would take us two trips, accelerating them up to speed individually, and we'd burn the last of our fuel and have to drift ballistically until the fleet caught up. We had barely enough supplies for that option.

Sighing, I asked everyone, "Any ideas? That contingency option would leave the fleet running lean for a hundred years after the two asteroids are mined out until a second mission could be attempted, at greater risk, in the asteroid belt almost three thousand years distant.

But in that scenario, the crews of the Cityships would be fully integrated into the Leviathan and the Cityships abandoned by then."

It certainly was a viable option, but another mission like this at twice the distance from the world would be needed at that time. Graz squeaked out at that, knowing the facts as well as the rest of us, "Well, in that scenario, at least we'd have three thousand years to prepare. What about the field the fleet will pass in four hundred years?"

Beta held her hand out and Graz buzzed from Rory's shoulder to alight there as Mother explained, "It wouldn't eliminate the problem of that future mission since there aren't many large asteroids in that belt, it seems to be debris torn from another astral body in some sort of cosmic collision billions of years ago. Though... the Cityship populations would be fully integrated by that time, leaving us in need of less fissionable materials."

Mac moved over to stand next to Rory, who hugged her arms to her, not feeling comfortable with the father who had abandoned her being that close. The close proximity of the ship and nobody else around to interact with has at least made it impossible for her to avoid him, and they were being civil now, which was an improvement. I saw it as just one baby step closer to some sort of reconciliation because the man loved her dearly and was at least trying.

Gah, was I rooting for them to be a family again? Maybe, but I'd settle for her letting him try to earn some semblance of forgiveness, not total forgiveness, but at least being a family again. And if it came down to me having to choose between them, then it would be, so long Oberon, it was nice knowing you.

He sighed, looking odd without the exoskeleton-assist frame he had worn before he was outed, making him look, I don't know, stouter, more sturdy? Or was that just his Oberon persona showing through the Mac-suit he wore? “Those bastard Outliers truly and fully fucked us. Leaving us two choices to survive. Either we do the unconscionable and leave the Cityships behind with all their population to die slowly in space, or we do these risky missions in an attempt to save us all.”

I blinked at how he just weighed them between his hands as if they were equal, but was relieved when he smiled sadly at all of us and finished, “So really there is no choice at all.” He looked around. “I think we should try to complete the primary mission here, we have the heart, the intelligence, and the wherewithal to try to work a miracle here. What say you all?”

I nodded and placed a hand over the table. Mother's was there on top of mine before I finished the movement. Then Mac joined in, Graz buzzing over to stand on our stacked hands. We all turned to Aurora, who was just staring at the three-dimensional representation of Morrigan, her brow creased in deep thought. I loved that look, knowing the mind behind it was staggeringly intelligent, which just made her that much more desirable to me. Smart women are hot. I may have a type.

"You really are a trickster, aren't you Morrigan?" she whispered.

"Love?" I asked.

That got her to tear her eyes away from the hologram for a moment, then she did a quick double-take when she saw all of us with our hands in. Aurora smiled and looked from us to the screens of data flowing. As that smile grew, she said, "The data is wrong. It is tricking us."

She reached over and absently placed her hand on top of her father's when Graz buzzed up a moment for her to do so before sitting on top of hers. Her attention was still split, as she said, "I'm in. And I think our odds of success are far above what the onboard computer is calculating."

We all reclaimed our hands and at the same time, Beta was complaining that "Data doesn't lie," I was asking, "What do you mean? We've been over it a million times."

She enlarged our asset screen for us all to look at as we gathered around her. "This is what all our calculations are based on." She highlighted the ship's engines, the debris defense laser, the specialized gear and magic enhanced explosive gear we brought with us, and the artifact itself. She even moved the Tug's mass as a gravity driver if it were to be used as an infinitesimal addition to our course correction algorithms.

She looked around almost as if she was asking for us to confirm what we all knew already. She chuckled and typed something and two humanoid shapes appeared in the inventory. One was almost a caricature of a Fae, looking suspiciously like Mac with drool hanging from his mouth, and the other a shining representation of Aurora herself.

She said primly, “Outside of the Queens of the Seelie and Unseelie courts, the two most magically powerful Greater Fae are here on the New Hope. If my... if Oberon's power is anywhere near the Queens' then we have almost doubled our demolition power. I'm feeling a little optimistic since we did the resource mapping of Morrigan.”

My eyes widened. I hadn't even thought of that. I've seen Rory blow blast doors out of bulkheads that were designed to take a meteor strike, and Oberon throwing lightning in space to cut through enemy ships. And for the first time since our data was compiled, I felt a smile creeping onto my lips.

“Game on,” I muttered, as Beta started playing a song called Invincible, by a singer named Pat Benatar from Doc's private cache of anthropological music.

Graz buzzed around the room, sifting sparkling dust behind her as she zipped to the window to look at the small barren world just below us. “Oh yeah, we're cuttin' you up you rock bastard!”

Mother corrected, “Morrigan was female, so the proper derogative would be bitch.”

“How am I supposed to know that? All you Bigs are the same to me.”

Mother ignored her and said to the group, “I just sent an updated, compressed data packet to the... umm to me... this is so weird. And we'll hear back from the powers that be if we are to continue with case alpha in about eight hours with the round trip time lag.”

I looked at Rory as she seemed to forget who she was talking to as the two Greater Fae started discussing harmonic magic frequencies and resonance patterns with the artifact. I smiled at the two intellectuals and didn't want to ruin it since my girl sounded so excited, so I pulled Beta to the corridor and down to the maintenance bay.

When she looked at me quizzically I prompted, “Let's go about calculating the best shear planes along the natural fault lines on this rock to get the mass down to something we can move in time, and if we do it right, maybe have it shaped well enough to fit back into your heart's sphere.”

Ok, are lifelike mechanical constructs supposed to look amused when you talk about their heart? With the Fae features she incorporated, it just made her look like a mischievous imp.

She just started projecting a multitude of possibilities she had already been working on. The biggest obstacle was that the composition of the asteroid hadn't been what our scientists had interpolated. Based on its projected mass, they had assumed Morrigan was what is known as a rubble pile asteroid, that was formed as many much smaller asteroids attracted to each other to build the asteroid up in layers like a snowball.

But now that we were here and got proper scans, it turns out that the composition was different than most of the asteroids in the debris field. The core of Morrigan was a solid chunk of rock and minerals, covered in a surface layer of rubble which likely formed as smaller asteroids were attracted to it. So it was more like a cheese log that was rolled in nuts than anticipated.

The detonation cords and magi-tech directed energy projectors would have accomplished our original goal in just about a week. But this... this was going to take a lot more finesse and power to accomplish, especially since we would be cutting off the main body which has a much larger diameter than the lobe we had originally been targeting.

We started mapping probable pressure and shock patterns, and what each detonation might do the to the asteroid's slow spin and trajectory. In most cases, the New Hope would need to be firing its main engines, pushing against the Morrigan with artifact magic assist to counter any adverse reactions. The only problem was trying to reliably predict how each fracture would act through varied materials.

If we had all of Mother's computing power to create endless simulations for a few months, we'd have a detailed roadmap of how to proceed, but for the most part, it was going to count on our best guesses and gut feelings. Something Graz and I took almost twenty minutes explaining to Beta.

Mother took the time to nod by the end of the first hour and share, “You've really got a knack for probabilities, Knith. Most of your... 'gut feelings'... have played out well in simulations. The only variable we don't know for sure is...”

Graz buzzed up in front of her eyes and blurted, “Just how much juice the bring your daughter to work twosome up there is capable of bringin' to bear.”

I shook my head. “I'm not going to interrupt them. It's the first time since we've been confined to such close quarters for four months that she's talking to the old man.”

“Well, you can count on Mac to have the power the Queens have. I mean, he had been the one to place that gaes on the entire Greater Fae population, including the Queens, so that they can't tell any lies. As far as I know, the old space pirate is the only one not affected by it,” Graz said.

I shook my head when Mother looked hopeful and countered, “I don't think so. From what I gather, he had almost died by expending his entire life force to pull it off. The Queens would never place themselves in danger of expending their life forces. And you can be sure of the fact that if the Summer and Winter Ladies ever pooled their power for the common good, they would be able to lift the curse easily.”

Graz sat on the workbench we had appropriated and nodded slowly. “And those two ever cooperating on something together would be the end of days and I would have officially seen everything.”

With a smirk, I said, “Where have you been since the Firewyrm incident? They've been doing almost everything together and acting like it is distasteful, but their body language says differently. I'll lay odds that they could lift the Gaes at any time, but they are leaving it in place because it amuses them. And it makes for a more exciting time to fool people while telling no lies.”

“Sooo... almost as powerful as one of the Ladies? And where does that put Princess Pucker up?”

I rolled my eyes and swatted at her, but she easily buzzed out of the way in time to hide behind one of Beta's pointed ears. “Watch it you flying rat, that's my girl you're talking about.”

Instinct had me spinning as I took a step back, my hand snagging one of my MMGs and raising it to between Mac's eyes when he began to speak right behind me, “She is... oh. Hello.”

I exhaled in exasperation as I holstered the weapon again and sputtered out, “Damn it, man! Don't sneak up on a girl like that!”

“I didn't, but exceptional reflexes, I've never seen a human move so fast. I can see why you vex the guards at Ha'Real now, Knith. I would have been hard-pressed to have stopped you if I had been so inclined.”

My defense was weak. “You did too.”

"No, he didn't," Beta, the living ship traitor said.

Graz started to speak, surely she had my back. "He just walked right up to you and you shat yourself."

Giving them the stink eye, I told the Captain of the Underhill, "You almost gave me a coronary. And if I had died, I would have spaced your ass."

He smirked, it was the same smirk he got when he was enjoying our weekly poker games before he had revealed himself. Then he said, his chest puffing with pride, "Of all my children, Au'Rothora, has benefited most from the well of power the Forge of Creation has bestowed upon her. Her well of potential expands faster than any before her. At such a young age, she already possesses about a tenth of the spark of my Mab, and may likely possess half of her power by the time we hit planet-fall, so she may become the next Winter Lady."

Blinking, I sputtered out one of Doc's odd sayings he got from the records of Earth culture from around the same time as the ancient music we enjoyed, "Whoa, whoa, whoa, be kind, rewind! Au'Rothora?"

I was smirking right up until a voice that sounded to similar to Mab's growled out with all the icy chill of Winter, "Papa!"

He winced, squinting one eye in apology, and she just huffed out in exasperation, "Many Humans had problems pronouncing our birth names before Exodus, so many of us simplified our names for them. That is why I am listed in the Worldship citizen database as Aurora."

I tried not to snort when Beta whispered to the air in amusement, "Not anymore." She was incorrigible. Her innocently coy smile when Rory glared at her was priceless.

I quickly got back on topic before something unfortunate happened, and we all found ourselves blown out into space or something since my girl did have just a wee bit of an explosive temper at times. "So we got ourselves a Mab or Titania with the two of you combined?"

Graz whistled. "That's a lot better than a poke with a sharp stick." She buzzed over to burrow into Rory's silky hair and poke her head out next to her ear as my girl reached up absently and patted the Sprite's head with her pinky.

To change the subject, the princess of the Unseelie Court asked, "What did you three abandon us to do down here?"

Beta supplied, "Mass mitigation of Morrigan. We've got all the tectonics worked out and the fracture and fault lines and the power required for each of three slices to bring us down to our target mass in time. We just didn't have the figures for the power input we could expect from your magics. And by what you shared, we are going to be pulling this one extremely close. Uncomfortably close."

The two Greater Fae scrolled through all our work, much faster than I would have ever been able to read, both nodding and grunting in appreciation of our work. I kept looking back and forth at them, realizing their mannerisms and physical ticks were unstintingly similar. Like father like daughter I guess.

Mac mused aloud to himself, “If only we had the Ya'Tesh Focus I gave Knith, we could amplify the...”

“What!?” Rory spat out. “You have the Ya'Tesh? That was supposed to have been destroyed when the Elves attempted a coup before the Fae Courts were formed. It's too dangerous. If someone were to use it with the Forge of Creation they could...”

He nodded. “And they did once upon a time, long before the Fae were created from raw magic of the artifacts leftover from the forge after it shattered, being amplified by the Ya'Tesh to forge our universe.”

I held up a hand, feeling extremely small, and out of my weight class as I prompted, “Uhh... are you talking about the Big Bang?”

Beta and Graz droned out together, “Obviously,” like I were the one kid in class who just didn't get the lesson.

“Oh.”

Rory grinned at me. “Yes, oh.”

Then before she could start arguing about the fact the man had this dangerous thing that apparently amplified the magic of creation, I held my hand up awkwardly again, feeling as though I were in school, and all the instructors knew more about life than I could ever hope to.

They all turned to me and I held up a finger as I dug in my belt pouches and grasped a small metal object and held it up. “Are you talking about the harmonica you gave me, Mac?”

Both their eyes bulged in panicked disbelief as Mac sputtered, “Why do you have that here? There's an artifact on board!”

Before I could answer, Rory asked in a careful, calm voice, “Umm... Knith, do you always have that on you?”

I nodded. “It's saved me a couple times already.”

Then she spun on Oberon and started yelling at him, making me wince again at how much she sounded like Mab just then, “We brought her into the Ka'Infinitum to experience it. And she had the Ya'Tesh Focus with her!? Are you completely insane!?”

“Hey now. How was I supposed to know she'd carry it around with her? I figured it would be safe with her because nobody would expect the Focus to be in the hands of a Human Enforcer.”

He was pale though and I paled too, recalling the Big Bang revelation earlier. I whispered, “Fuck me sideways and space me naked.” Then I tried to hand the harmonica to Mac then Rory, both of them recoiled in a panic so I sighed and put it back in my pouch as I muttered to them, “Oh sure, let me just hang onto this universe killing focus thing. No pressure.”

Then they exhaled in relief once it was out of sight, then he started to chuckle, low and slow, picking up speed until Rory joined in. Soon we were all laughing, releasing all the tension that had just built to titanic proportions just a moment earlier.

We weren't insane, not at all. I was going to throw up.

Then Oberon, being the first to compose himself looked at the fault lines and said as he looked at my belt pouch-like he could see the harmonica, “Well, we've got all the power we need to expedite this. I suggest we follow the plan for bisecting Knith and Mother have laid out here.”

CHAPTER 11

Put Some Spin On It

That's how we wound up pushing the prow of the New Hope against Morrigan's surface, just twelve hours later, after getting updated orders from the Leviathan.

I looked around the bridge as Mac, for no reason other than just to prove what we already knew, fired the main engines for a three-second burn. Besides the groaning of the superstructure of the New Hope, Morrigan was unimpressed. The effect on her was so negligible that the decimal places that displayed on the flight path of the asteroid may well have been an immovable object or an irresistible force.

With a sardonic grin, I let a question drift about us, “Is it just me, or are we all just a little nuts? We're supposed to fly this thing like a ship on a trajectory that has to be within ten-thousandths of a degree of accuracy.”

My girl, in a rare form of guile and scoundrel-osity, shrugged and said as she flicked a finger between Oberon and herself where Graz sat on her shoulder, “We're Fae, we don't know what your excuses are.” She winged a thumb at Beta and me.

That was as unnerving as it was humorous. I hoped it was such a nonanswer since it didn't directly address my words that she could be so flippant, but since Fae couldn't lie it put a question to me, did the Fae act so erratic because they have lived so long they were slowly losing it? I mean, just look at Mab. Then again, how sane are any of us anyway? Isn't it all just a matter of perspective and what the majority would deem normal?

I shook my head, wondering why I always have such existential thoughts at the most inappropriate times? Sighing I asked, "You kiss your girl with that mouth?"

She beamed like a Faun in zero-g as she glided my way, mischief on her lips and twinkling in her eyes as she purred, "Why yes I do, Knith Shade." Everyone else groaned as she started to lean in, her eyes on my lips, she paused and shot the room the stink eye. "You're all just jealous, go get your own Enforcer to kiss." They groaned again as she stole a quick kiss from me. I just beamed in delight.

Beta looked uncomfortable and started playing with the controls on the bridge. I really needed to talk to her. Then as if she knew my attention was on her... well she did since I was in my armor, she changed the subject. "I've been analyzing the data, and have determined that the loose debris on the surface of Morrigan has an average depth of five feet. Much deeper in some areas and virtually nonexistent in others."

We all turned to her and she shrugged. "It accounts for almost five percent of the mass of the asteroid." She left it hanging.

Graz picked up the thread. "Ooo... so if there was a way to strip it away, like the seed tufts of a humming crystal cottonweed, it would be easier to fly away with it. We'd only need to extricate less of the actual asteroid then, or go with the lighter weight as a safety margin."

Mac nodded, scratching his chin as Aurora said with wide appreciative eyes, "You never cease to amaze, Mother, that's brilliant." Then she hesitated and asked though the side of her mouth, as her eyes flicked up in her thinking mode, "Umm... any ideas?"

I pointed at the ship's controls and made an exploding motion with my hands. Beta patted the top of my head in a teasing manner. "Good idea, Knith, but we don't have either the time or fuel to use the engine backwash vaporize or blow away almost a hundred square miles of surface area."

Crossing my arms across my chest I muttered, "Not all of us can calculate that sort of thing in a millisecond, lady."

All the other hands went up as the three traitors said, "I did."

I was going to concede then spun to point at Graz, with her fairy-shit eating grin on. "You as so full of shit."

She shrugged and said like an indignant teen, "Prove it."

Mac asked, "Atmosphere?"

Rory caught his line of questioning. "Virtually undetectable. So laminar particle flow generation is a no go." Did she mean wind?

"Gravitic desublimation?" she asked.

"Too massive for even our combined potential. Only localized areas with the same time limitations as Knith's plan."

My plan? It was only a question.

"How are you with polymer potential constructs?" He asked.

"I helped mother contain the hull breaches in after the Outlier coup attempt."

I whispered to Beta, "Is it just me or do these two make magic sound as if it's just science and physics?"

Mother surprised me by nodding and teasing, "I know, it's sort of pleasingly stimulating, isn't it? She could wind up my new favorite."

I turned to her, mouth wide in shock. "Mother!"

She giggled. "You're my number one, Knith. But seriously, magic is just physics that scientists just haven't figured out yet. The Greater Fae understand it at an instinctual level, and as science slowly catches up, the more the principals can be replicated with that new understanding."

I noticed that the back and forth had stopped between my girl and her father and they were looking at us. Rory prompted, "Have you not noticed that most magic follows your understanding of physics for the most part? Such as the conservation of matter and energy. Energy cannot be created nor destroyed?"

Graz zipped up to me, eating a dried berry. Where had that come from? She sat on the rim of my helmet, "That's why there are two courts. Divided by the way their magic potentials harvest the energy to bend it to their will."

She licked her fingers one at a time as I contemplated what she was trying to say. My eyes went wide with comprehension, and both Mac and Rory had appreciative looks on their faces at that epiphany. “I'm not slow. This stuff was never taught in any of the classes I had, not even at the college level.” I pointed out.

They nodded as Mac said, “Only the top physics theorists are delving into that very concept. Some think of string theory as some sort of unifying concept, but that is a simplified look at how we Fae interact with the universe and beyond. And some have come to theorize that the very universe we live in is some sort of magical construct, but are at a loss to find the causal link. The Forge of Creation. You are the only human to have witnessed it and know of its origins and still live.”

Was there a hint of warning in his tone?

So I just inclined my head at the expectant Fae and prompted as my mind whirred. “So the extreme cold and heat of each Court... it isn't the magic, it is a result of the magic? The Winter Court pulls energy from the matter around them as energy, chilling everything around them, and the Summer? Exciting the particles around them and harvesting the heat generated as energy?”

Aurora looked at her father. “I told you she had a mind as formidable as her fighting ability. It is why she has the highest case closure record in the Brigade. She takes on the enemy with both her mind and her brawn.”

I almost started beaming at the praise but realized we had once again been derailed. "So, polymer potential constructs? Force fields I presume? How could they help? And how could she encase the entire asteroid? My girl is good, but that good? Not even you, Mab, or Titania could do that."

The Maiden of Winter smiled as she seemed to catch his line of thought. "Ah, just a wedge in front of the vessel. But how long can you weather the vacuum? Most Greater Fae last ten to fifteen minutes before they are frozen enough to lose mobility, twenty hours to be frozen solid. Mother's last test gave me three times that."

What? The Winter Lady tests to see how long her children can survive vacuum? Then I contemplated her words, she could be exposed to vacuum for around a half-hour before succumbing to it and floating endlessly, frozen but aware for eternity?

That made me contemplate Sindri. He had covertly hired some Remnants to fly out to retrieve his body once his sentence of spacing was carried out. It had taken them three hours to do so. So at least he did suffer that long. I'm not normally a vindictive person and wouldn't wish that on anyone under normal circumstances, but the bastard had cut my eggs out of me and tried to kill me... more than once, so I was ok with my venom on this topic.

Rory must have read this all in my face as she shot me a concerned look, and Graz even buzzed up to pat my nose.

Mac looked impressed and proud of his daughter then said almost sheepishly, “I can withstand the rigors of a vacuum for around twenty-four hours, twice that if I bring atmosphere with me.”

Her eyes bulged as she repeated, “Bring atmosphere with... that's inspired! I've never thought to do that. Mother will be in for a surprise the next time she throws me in an airlock.”

“Agreed then?” he asked.

She nodded and turned to us expectantly. I exhaled in frustration and admitted, “I've no clue what you're planning.”

Graz tittered. “You don't see what they're up to?”

“No, and neither do you.”

“I do too.”

“Prove it.”

“Well, they're going to... vacuum and stuff.”

“Idiot.”

“Null.”

Mother tutted, “Children.”

We stopped feeling properly embarrassed. My eyes widened as I looked at her face, which got more and more expressive every day.

I sputtered out with a smile to Rory, “You better tell us all your plan because Mother doesn't have a clue either!”

Beta complained, “Most of my core is inside of me four light hours out. I only have a few hundred times the computing capacity as your squishy gray stuff in your head.”

“Brains?”

“That's the word.” She was smirking and I shoved her shoulder. She not only looked Fae, but her avatar construction was as sturdy as one as I was the one who moved with my shove, not her.

Aurora said, “If you two are done. I just need to deflect any debris from the ship as Papa deals with the rubble covering the surface. Mother, we're going to need you to fly, Oberon needs to be outside the ship to sling the energy needed.”

Then I got it. After he was spaced by the Outliers he had made it to the Leviathan, slinging lightning that destroyed everything in its path. We were going to fly along the surface while he laid waste to the surface of Morrigan, and Rory would protect us from debris. After blinking in shock, I thought of the fuel supplies and asked, “How wide can you sling that energy? Won't we burn too much fuel that way too?”

He grinned. “I'm not needed to destroy the rubble, just displace it enough for its own inertia to break free of the gravity of the asteroid. So, a swath about a half-mile wide should do it. I'd have to be outside for a couple hours. The fuel expenditure would be negligible.”

I blinked at that then shook my head. “You can just use the EVA suits that were provided for the mission.”

Rory answered for him, shaking her head. “He would destroy the gloves of the suit, rendering it useless for the same reason he can't do it from inside the bridge here. The energy originates from his hands, it isn't projected at a distant point like some magics.”

"Oh." Then I asked the universe, "Why the fuck can't just one thing be simple in this godforsaken mission?" There was no divine answer from any of the multitudes of gods worshiped by the various cultures and races on the world. Of course not. I exhaled in exasperation, then asked in real concern, "Does it hurt? Decompression?"

He nodded and said brightly with a smirk, "Excruciating, and then there's the panic of trying to breathe nonexistent air, but then your body becomes accustomed to it and it isn't so bad as you slowly lose body heat by infrared radiation since convection and conduction don't work in space."

I knew that part, even the human body takes hours to freeze solid in space since you only lose body heat by infrared radiation. But the rest was horrifying, and he was willing to do it anyway. I saw I wasn't alone, Rory didn't look happy at all about it but looked resigned to it too.

"You know, we don't need to do this at all?" I asked. "We have a solid plan."

Mac nodded. "Yes, but it is predicated on everything going just right. If we can give ourselves some metaphorical breathing room. Then it would behoove us to attempt it."

I prompted Beta from the bridge an hour later, "You good to do this? You glitched a half hour ago and panicked."

She looked at me sardonically and said, "Of the two of us, who can fly a million-ton tug vessel better even if my components are having difficulties in the radiation? It is happening less now that we left the high-rad band."

I sighed. "I'm not that bad of a pilot, I ride a Tac-Bike and have even flown Brigade Transports, and have dozens of hours on the simulator in the..."

Graz blurted, "I've got my chit tokens on Mother. You crashed the simulator as often as you didn't, Knith."

Grr. Fine, maybe I wasn't as skilled with larger vessels as I was on my Tac-Bike, which I could fly like an extension of myself. I flipped them off and looked over to Aurora, who was looking nervously out the blast windows to the surface of Morrigan we were backing away from to get into position to spiral around it for Mac.

I stepped to her side, laying a hand on her shoulder, and she absently reached up to put her hand on mine. "You ok, love? You look nervous. We can still call this off."

She shook her head. No, I'm just a little anxious. I've never done a prolonged projection this long before. I usually anchor my shields onto an anchor point. But the concept of this is not to keep something in or out, it's to stop things from impacting us. And if I anchor it to the hull, then the impacts would be translated through the shield to the superstructure. So I need to project it out in front of us and absorb the kinetic strikes myself.

"And that's giving you this anxiety?" I knew her, and how Fae Magic was based on the strength and will of the caster. And my girl was strong, and her will was next to unbreakable. So...

"Is it Mac? Don't worry about him, ok? I've seen first hand him standing outside the world on the skin, and throwing raw power through the enemy. He can do this."

She tilted her head back, closed her eyes, and said in a tired, frustrated tone, "I know. And he's as you would put it, a child abandoning son of a bitch, but..."

"He's your dad."

She opened her eyes and nodded in resigned humor. "He's my dad."

We heard steps on the hull above us, then three stomps, Graz flew over and stomped her feet on the control screen and the external camera view of the beautifully perfect Fae form of Oberon stood there, in defiance of the vacuum around him, the most hostile environment in existence, his eyes starting to crackle with blue electricity, as the same started to arc between his fingers as he spread them wide before him.

I hear my own voice whisper, "Wow."

My girl nodded, eyes wide.

I had a thought and asked, "From which court does Oberon come from? I mean, he doesn't seem to be using Winter or Summer magic."

She said offhandedly, "Well, he's Oberon. Neither court. He's... something else." Then she got back on point. "Here goes nothing."

She raised a hand and said, "Begin the flight when my shield forms please, Mother."

Beta just nodded once, her eyes trained on the readouts before her, and I knew she likely had hundreds of other data streams feeding her information on all the ship's systems, the status of the Asteroid, and all the external camera and scanner feeds.

Rory's eyes went white with that blue frost fire burning in them, the cabin went almost ten degrees cooler in a moment and the floor and walls iced up, then she thrust her palm outward and a crackling field of blue energy formed in a wedge in front of the tug. Ice crystals that I knew were actually physically frozen magic potential formed in space around the shield.

A moment later we went into motion and silent lightning streaked to the surface of the asteroid. At first, it was violently blowing away the layer of debris and rubble, vaporizing most and scoring the solid rock beneath it. He seemed to pull back, the power of the lightning diminished and spread to blanket more area of the surface as we moved on the slow, spiraling path.

The lightning was now more subtle as it struck, almost burrowing and causing the rubble to float away, some still being flung or reduced to atoms if it passed through the lightning itself. And the tug began to shake in time with how Rory's arm was being slammed back like a shock absorber, over and over.

She leaned into it and her other hand thrust forward like she was pausing against a wall, a leg moving back to give her more leverage. I felt useless. I wanted to help shore her up, but at least I was cognizant enough, watching this impossible sight, to know that she'd lose power the longer I held onto her, so I dutifully stayed away.

I did the only thing I could. I watched the data, only after I told her, “You don't know how sexy you are when you're being all badass like this, Rory.”

She smirked and I swear her power flared brighter. Graz was just sitting on the console, looking at me like I were obtuse. I told her, “Shut up.” And then just watched as a half-mile wide swath of the asteroid was cleared of rubble. It was like watching a cloud of rocks and pebbles floating away from the surface.

I moved to the window to witness it with my own eyes instead of watching it on the screens. Seeing something like this firsthand always put the recordings to shame. You can't capture the impossibility of such an awe-inspiring sight and the emotional component it instills in you in a recording. Graz landed on my shoulder and just whispered in awe, her eyes bulging, “Mother fairy humper.”

I nodded my agreement.

We had circled Morrigan three times, clearing over half the rubble, when proximity alarms started sounding, and Beta seemed to be having problems at the helm, making dozens of corrections by hand until she just dropped the controls and stood. She cocked her head and all the controls started operating themselves as we made yet another course correction.

By the time we had circled another orbit and a half, Aurora was calling out, “Mother? What are you doing? This is getting hairy out there, it's hard to track the incoming debris.”

Beta sounded frustrated as she said, “There is an unanticipated anomaly occurring because of the detritus elimination process.”

“An anomaly, what is it?” I blurted.

She said as she made another course correction through her link to the ship. “It is introducing a transaxial spin in the mass, that is increasing more rapidly as more of the rocky body of the asteroid is exposed to the radiation from the nebula, heating its exterior.”

Oh, space me now. “Display anomaly please.” The console by Graz and I bloomed, showing the original rotation of the asteroid being on a singular axis and stabilized as it settled into it over the millions of years it has been on its current course. But now there was another spin being introduced that was at about a fifty-degree angle from the native axis, introducing a heavy wobble in the massive chunk of space rock.

“Does this affect our bisection mission? What about geologic stresses or ejection vectors?” I asked.

“I've been modeling it as fast as I can, I don't have all my resources available to me this far from my core. Seventy-three percent of the simulations so far show a probability for success, and that number is starting to drop the more of the asteroid is exposed,” she replied.

"What will those probability factors be if we complete this?" Aurora asked.

"Fifty-seven percent."

"We need to stop, now!" I blurted.

And Beta took that literally and fired all the maneuvering thrusters, causing the roar of those engines to fill the space as I was thrown against the forward window since my mag boots hadn't been engaged.

My face smashed against the glass gave me a front-row seat to seeing a shocked looking Oberon as he tumbled past in space toward Morrigan. He struck Rory's shield and it wrapped around him like a cocoon. I looked back at her as I regained my footing as we came to a dead stop relative to the asteroid.

She had one hand curled into a loose fist like she was holding a small animal in it, and her other hand was being thrust forward as I felt the shaking and undulation of the last of the ejected material bouncing off her shield so it could tumble out into space.

I was already running to the ladders before she released the shield. "Get him close to the airlock," I called out.

She nodded, and I realized she had a sheen on her forehead, she had been sweating and it was a frozen sheet of ice on her face, making her look ethereal. This had been stressing her power more than she was letting on. Fuck. I went faster. Beta was curling around in my head by the time I hit the lower deck running, and she started re-configuring my armor into EVA mode before I even asked for it.

Graz had buzzed ahead and slammed the airlock controls with her feet, using her minuscule weight and momentum to press the button. She buzzed into my helmet just as the visor snicked into place and I slammed my hand back on the door control as I entered the airlock. Then I stood on the door, engaging my mag boots as Mother hit the override and the outer doors opened, causing explosive decompression.

I held for a fraction of a second until I could see a cocooned Oberon about a hundred meters from the ship and disengaged the boots, allowing the last of the escaping air to fling me out at speed faster than I could run.

Graz was yelling, “We're all going to diiiiiiiiiiiii...”

I pulled my arms in and just glided toward him. I was going to use the new capabilities of my EVA mode to correct my trajectory when he was moved directly in front of us, Beta must have been guiding Rory.

“...iiiiii... oh hey, that was pretty neat... iiiieeee.”

We hit Mac like a street cleaner drone, and he grabbed my waist with a grip that could rend steel alloy. I thought about slowing and stopping relative to the New Hope and maneuvering to the airlock, my armor followed my commands with its new maneuvering capabilities. Small thrusts of inert gasses expelled from various points on my armor and flew us steadily back to the open airlock door.

The moment we cleared the hull, Mother slammed the door down and repressurized. When all the indicators showed equalized pressure a moment later, my visor flicked up and Graz buzzed up into Oberon's face. “Mac! You ok?”

He looked sluggish but held a finger up as he bent at his waist, hands on his knees, then a moment later he gasped and took in a huge lungful of air. “There. That wasn't so bad now, was it? It's just the remembering how to breathe thing that gets me every time. Now, will someone explain to me just what in the seven rings of Chronos just happened?” he gasped.

CHAPTER 12

Easy as Pie

Before we could fill Mac in on the new twist, pun intended, to our mission, we all sat back and relaxed for a bit to gather our wits around us in the kitchen area where we could get some calories into the magic users while Graz and I ate a light lunch.

Rory had shaken off a look of panic and wonder at me when they met us down by the airlock, then proceeded to chastise me about my reckless behavior. "Mother could have guided me to bring him back to the airlock."

"Well, how was I supposed to know that? I saw the man tumbling through space and I acted on instinct." I pouted.

She warmed at that and caressed my cheek, that slight bit of wonder back in her eyes as she said, "And without any hesitation at all." Then she got a little cross. "You could have been hurt. I'm just glad you are ok."

Graz buzzed her wings. "Umm... hello? What about me? I was there too."

Rory rolled her eyes and lifted her on her palm to kiss the top of her head. "Of course brave Sprite."

I cocked an eyebrow and reached over and mimed zipping Graz's lips. She gave me a glare and just crossed her arm over her chest.

Mac was moving sluggishly. “Can we continue this in the mess? Staving off the effects of vacuum on my person burns a lot of calories, and recovery is slow without replenishment.”

So that's how we wound up eating our mid-day meal in relative silence as Beta projected the now wobbling asteroid on the wall. After each bite, the smartass Sprite would unzip her lips for the next bite before re-zipping them. Fine, she was pretty damn funny.

I was keeping one eye on Mac's hands, which had looked severely burned when we first got him back on board. His healing had been progressing slowly, almost immeasurably a first, but the more food he ate the faster the healing progressed. And by the time we were done eating, he looked unharmed but just a little more tired than I was used to seeing.

Taking in the dampened mood, I decided that it was counterproductive so pointed out on the readouts beside the floating three-dimensional projection. “The asteroid mass was reduced by three percent by that attempt. So we have less mass to bisect from the main body now.”

Beta squashed my attempt to inject a little positivity into the room. “The probability of controlled bisection success is now at seventy-two percent. Less than optimal. There is always Engineer Hangzhou's Plan Epsilon. If we run out of time and don't wish to settle for targets Beta and Gamma.”

We all blurted out, Graz unzipping her lips to join in, “No!”

I took a deep breath to center myself and then explained in a calm, collected voice. “It isn't a plan, never is 'Nuke the Fairy humper!' a plan. Sane and rational people do not detonate nuclear engine cores on an astral body that contains fissionable materials.”

She looked around and everyone slowly nodded as they tried to deduce if she was serious or not. She shrugged an apology. “He just seemed so very enthusiastic about that course of action.”

Graz sighed and flew up to pat her cheek. “Oh, Mother. Hangzhou was also calling it an invasion. I think the unstable Big hadn't slept for over a week. Then again, Satyrs be crazy during the rutting season. So...” She shrugged, leaving it hanging and zipped away as Beta swatted at her.

Rory covered her mouth to cover her smile, which just got me grinning and Mac snorting at the pout on Beta's lips. It was amazing how expressive Mother's avatar's face was. Then everyone cracked up in nervous laughter as Graz spun in the air, sending sparkling dust drifting down as she said, “I think I'll adapt that as my new life motto, Knith. Never is 'Nuke the Fairy humper!' a plan.”

Mother just crossed her arms over her chest, looking so much like Rory did when she was pouting, but then broke into a smile and joined in our cathartic laughter.

I walked around, cleaning up and placing the trays and utensils into the sonic cleaner, then turned to stare at our adversary, wobbling there in space like a drunk Leprechaun at a New Year's Eve gala in the B-Rings. “So what did this do to our timeline?”

Beta highlighted the optimum shear planes, there were the same three, modified slightly to account for the cast-off trajectories with the augmented spin of the asteroid. “The bad news is that the deployment of the detonation cords and magi-tech directed energy projectors is going to take longer now, by approximately eighteen hours. The good news is that we gained a day as ninety percent of the rubble and regolith along those shear planes have already been cleared so less drilling will be needed for the anchors.”

I brightened. That's right! The corkscrew path we flew when we attempted the debris ejection began along those paths. I smiled and said, “So we've gained six hours.”

Graz winged a thumb toward me from where she hovered by the two Greater Fae. “The null can do math. Should we give her a gold star?”

She gleeped and grinned cheesily when she turned back to see I had moved up to her and was staring her down from inches away. She said through the fake toothy grin, “I mean... oh, yes, she's right.” I reached up, pinched her wings, dangled her in front of a squinted eye, then winked at her and placed her on my shoulder.

Aurora took charge, sounding confident, and commanding, and unnervingly like Queen Mab. “Ok, playtime's over. Let's get serious. Papa, please land us on the primary sheer plane, please. Knith, prepare the detonation cords, Mother and I will handle the directed energy projectors.”

“Why am I on demolition? I can...” I asked.

"Because, love, the projectors weigh fifteen hundred pounds each, and four of them need to be placed along each shear plane."

Looking from her to my gauntlets I pointed out. "I may not be as strong as you or Mother's glamour doll body here, but I do have powered armor, remember? And it's close to zero-g out there, anyway."

She sighed at me, shaking her head as Beta cocked a brow. "Glamour doll?"

Graz piped up, "Yeah, you're hot, own it."

Then Rory explained. "Your scatter armor is impressive, true. But it only enhances your own physical strength, which, while at the top end of what the Human body is capable of... by design... would not be adequate to the task, even in zero-g, without burning through the power cells at an alarming rate as you move that much mass around, controlling its inertia. If you drain your armor, then you'll need to use the spare EVA suit they placed on board for the remainder of the mission."

She purred, looking at my lips and licking hers, which reminded me of how sexually frustrated I've been these long weeks on the New Hope. It wasn't like we could sneak away anywhere onboard to work out that frustration. She continued in that purr. "Papa, Mother, and I can move the projectors even in full gravity. So you..." She kissed the tip of my nose. "...are on demolition duty."

Fine. I voiced my thought. "Fine. I do like a girl with a lot of muscle." Then I furrowed my brow. "Just what are you using to power yourself, Beta, if you are that much stronger than me but your power won't be drained."

She said coyly, answering like a Fae, "I may have access to technology not yet available to the Brigade." She looked a little smug, and I realized it was because she was listening to my surface thoughts again. I thought to her with a mirror of her smugness, "I always thought you'd be a redhead, but I see you're more Fae than just in looks."

She answered in my head, "I thought you liked the Greater Fae."

I closed my eyes and sighed. She confirmed why her Beta form was different than her other avatars with that. I thought back to her, "You didn't need to choose your form just to please me, Mother. I love you in any form. You're my world, literally."

"But you chose Aurora."

I sighed in frustration. "I love her differently, but nobody can take your place. You are the one who always has my back and I have yours. You and I are family, always have been."

She turned to look at me, she still struck me as an amalgam of Mir and Rory's physical makeup. She truly was stunning, and I wished I could see her the way she wanted me to.

She gave me a sad, but understanding smile, and I realized Rory and Graz were just looking between us. Graz squished her lips to one side of her face and spoke behind her hand to Rory like we couldn't hear her, "They're doing that communicating through the helmet interface thing again." Then to Beta and me, "Get a room."

Rory giggled at that as I swatted at Graz, who just buzzed out of my reach, giggling herself.

We all knew we were just stalling. So I sighed heavily and as I stepped casually out the door, the way Mac went and said, as I hit the door control, “Last one to the maintenance bay is a Fairy fart!” Then I ran, hearing them exclaiming loudly about me cheating as they opened to the door to follow.

I wish I could say that I won, but no matter the gravity, nobody can beat a buzzing Sprite. I don't think that Graz even used the ladders and corridors because I don't remember her passing me, but there she was, leaning on top of the det-cord crates when I slid to a stop, Rory and Mother elbowing each other for third place. I'm pretty sure Graz is using the ventilation shafts to navigate the ship.

Then we went to work, laying out the gear we'd need for each of the bisections, setting it up for rapid deployment. Well rapid as far as the projectors, the directional, magic enhanced shaped charges on the cord were going to take a day and a half each to circle the target zones since it would have to be done manually.

I looked up. “Wait a minute. We all trained in the simulations on all the components and systems for the mission. Am I going to get stuck schlepping across an asteroid while you two get to ride around in the tug from location to location?”

“Pretty much.” Mother said.

Rory giggled at that and leaned her head onto Beta's shoulder, holding onto her arm. “Mother, I wish you hadn't had to hide away from us for so long. You're positively wicked, and I would love to have been your friend all this time."

Then she corrected the tin smartass as she said, "We'll trade off in shifts after the projectors are set up."

"And we can gain even more mission time since I can walk, securing det-cord through your sleep cycles since I need no sleep." Beta shared.

Graz flew up to hover in front of us, rubbing her palms together in a sweeping, dismissing motion, "Easy as pie."

I poked her in the sternum and smirked. "Easy for you to say, you'll have a great view of us from the bridge."

"Go space yourself, Knith. We're partners, I'm going out there with you. I'll be your second set of eyes. I can watch the updates while you concentrate on not making us dead on a derelict space rock."

I sighed, knowing I wouldn't win, so I just resigned myself to knowing she'd be talking my ears off as I trudged across that derelict space rock. I silently thanked Mother for making sure I had a few terabytes of music I could drown the buzzing nuisance out with.

Was it wrong that I was getting excited to step onto a small world that nobody has ever set foot on before?

CHAPTER 13

Fire In The Hole

Ok, the excitement didn't last long. Don't get me wrong, when Mac set us down at the coordinates for the first magi-tech directed energy projector, Rory, and I were dumbstruck in awe when we stepped out onto an alien world in our EVA suits, the micro thrusters in my modded armor firing to keep my feet on the surface, her own magic keeping her feet firmly on the rock. My mag boots wouldn't work here for the same reason we couldn't use mag-sleds to move the equipment on the surface, as they both require metallic surfaces or Fae augmented materials and alloys designed to work with magnetic fields.

Graz voiced our amazement as she whispered from inside my helmet, her hands and face pressed up against the visor, “Woooooooow.” The breathless combination of the wondrous and foreboding holding us all in place as we took in the ancient world of rock which had been scored and lash marked by the raw power of Oberon's compressed magic lightning. Arching curved stalagmites of melted stone, which had cooled from impacts billions of years ago, causing the surface to look as though it was a graveyard of bones from creatures of unimaginable size.

The perpetual darkness of space was riddled with millions of bright pricks of light from the stars, more dazzling than diamonds in one direction, and the nebula's majesty on the other, its colorful glow lending an eerie glow to the nightmarish landscape. Only that dimly illuminated glow, and the absolute pitch black of the shadows were visible as far as the eye could see to the horizon less than a half mile away.

It took Beta stepping out beside us to snap us out of it. She carried the tools we'd need to anchor the projector as she stopped to stare up at the endless expanse, and said, “I've always believed I was so very massive, housing all my millions of charges, keeping them safe on the flight to a new world, containing your lives inside of me. But seeing this, seeing the majesty of the universe with eyes instead of sensors and cameras as I always have... I feel so very... small.”

I just nodded and reached over to lay a hand on her EVA suited arm, letting her know that even though we were all so insignificant at the scale we were witnessing, we still all had each other.

When we were training for the mission, I had asked Doc about the EVA suit he had modified for Beta. “Can't she survive the rigors of space? She doesn't have any organic components.”

He had pointed out, “Yes she can. The avatar she built for herself is far superior to the Human body, and even cutting edge when looking at all the magi-tech mods available to people now, if I'm reading the data right. But even though she's smarter, faster, and stronger than us, none of that will keep her from just floating off into space with her first step on an asteroid with micro-gravity.”

“Ah, point taken.” Sometimes I wonder why I don't contemplate a situation before opening my pie-hole at times like that. And since she didn't need oxygen or any life support systems, she could carry enough compressed gas propellant to walk the surface of Morrigan for over a week without replenishing her tank.

It hadn't taken a genius to hear the forlorn admiration he had for Mother and her avatar as he sighed out, “My girl is amazin', don't ya think?” I had just nodded my agreement as I beamed a smile at him.

Now here we were on this world that was just a concept in my mind weeks before, like the idea of old Earth and Open Air and the Ground. Something I only have heard about in stories and history lessons. This was... this was no longer a concept, this was real, and my mind just boggled as I looked around. This asteroid, no matter how alien it looked to me, would be the new Heart of the Leviathan... Mother's heart, and that thought made the small world we stood on less menacing for some reason.

I voiced that, my tone taking on a bit of reverence, “This will be your new Heart, Mother.”

Beta sighed. “It's beautiful.”

Rory spoke in an apologetic tone. “Right then, let's get to work, shall we? The sooner we finish, the sooner we can get back home.”

That got us into motion.

I helped to secure the projector with molecular fusing bolts we sank into the rough stone surface. Then we hooked up the det-cord to a port on it and I fired the first anchor pin to secure the first shaped charge to the surface, calibrated and then Rory hefted the spool onto the hard point connections that the nano-panels of my Scatter Armor formed at a thought.

She patted my back then when I turned to her, she pressed our helmets together and just stared into my eyes for a moment, then kissed where our visors touched. “Off you go then. Be careful, I love you.”

My heart sang and I'm sure I had a goofy look on my face as I did my coms check. “Shade, New Hope.”

Mac responded, “I read you loud and clear, Knith. Godspeed, we'll see you in six hours at the secondary.”

“Roger that.” I sighed, then made my girl giggle and gleep when I swatted her butt lightly before I started trudging off along the shear plane highlighted in my heads-up display with a seven hundred pound backpack on, the det-cord reeling out behind me for me to secure every seventy feet along the path.

Graz called out over coms, “No, don't everyone wish me luck too or anything. It's not like I'm also here. Oh wait... I am. Dumb Bigs.”

I assured her, “We love you too, you flying terror.”

“As it should be.” I had to hand it to the pint sized stowaway, she was pretty damn funny at times.

It is amazing just how much ordinance I was carrying. It was enough to destroy a Worldship with its magic assist to the explosives, and then on top of that, the projectors catch the subsurface shock-waves and amplified them all around the asteroid, to crack the astral body like a proverbial egg. Well at least that was the plan when we thought it would be one clean cut, shearing off the node with all the available projectors. But now, having to shear off much more expansive slices, we were relegated to splitting the projectors amongst three targets.

Even with the power of the artifact we brought along, we probably wouldn't have succeeded, but with the added power of Rory and Oberon and the Focus I'm not supposed to have, we might really succeed.

I turned back when Beta said in my head, “Knith?” She pointed and said, “There's the rest of me.” I looked skyward as the stars rotated slowly around us and a tiny, dim speck of light was highlighted. Data scrolled by it but I didn't pay much attention as I just blinked while my heart surged. Home. And we could see her from here because she was so massive. The Leviathan was the most magnificent sight in the universe.

I could almost hear a blush in her words as she said, “Thank you, someone has to be, so why not me.” I chuckled at her familiar joke. Then I sighed and started on the long walk, firing an anchor every seventy feet, and Graz doing my coms checks every fifteen minutes.

And as I said, the excitement and wonder of walking on the surface of a foreign world quickly wore off after the first half mile. And even though I was in micro gravity, and my armor was doing most of the work, it was hard work walking with the spool on my back. Mass was mass and I still had to move it and stop its momentum whenever I stopped or turned. The repetitive twisting and bending down to fire an anchor was going to leave my muscles aching.

Anticipating me, Beta started playing in my helmet a song from the anthropological section called Manic Monday, by a band called the Bangles. It was apropos and I muttered, “Very funny, lady,” as I trudged along.

My enhanced eyesight was a bonus, now that we were experiencing the surface conditions of Morrigan, I could still see in the near absolute darkness of the shadows I passed through when the terrain blocked the light of the nebula, the stars were enough illumination for me to make my way.

As I was handing off the det-cord pack to Beta once I reached the second projector, I was dead tired. She said almost cheerfully, “See you at the tertiary site in six hours, everyone, have a pleasant sleep.”

And we did. We were all exhausted from a hard day's work, and we only had to repeat this three more times for this bisection, then we'd move on to the second shear plane then the third. When I say we, I mean Rory, Graz and I. Oberon didn't seem to be tired at all, and tracked Mother's progress through the night cycle of the tug.

I walked the next leg when we woke to Mother trudging up to the third projector. I was able to get half way to close the loop too before the tug flew in and I was relieved for another sleep cycle. We were awoken when mother reached the first projector again.

Once the loop was closed by connecting the det-cord to the other port on the projector. Mac took us to a safe distance from Morrigan. Then Oberon took my harmonica, the Focus, and he and Rory grasped hands, their power building causing the lights to dim and the hair on my neck to stand on end,

Beta pulled up the detonation sequence on the main control console, and entered the arming codes, and released the safeties. Then she flicked up the cover on the little red button on top of the joystick yoke and looked around. She looked on my shoulder, “Would you like the honors, Graz?”

The Sprite brightened, a look of excitement on her face as she buzzed over, nodding emphatically, “You betcha!” Then she asked everyone? “Ready?” Our two Greater Fae, with Oberon in his true form just inclined their heads, a halo of magic around them, and Graz buzzed down at full speed, slamming the button with both feet as she squealed out, “Fire in the hole!”

CHAPTER 14

Tectonic Shifting

A clear tone rushed out of the Harmonica. I watched as their magic seemed to coalesce around the entire asteroid, around the first bisection plane. And as the note died out, I saw the silent plume of dust and rocky debris as what amounted to hundreds of tiny magic enhanced high explosives went off, causing a halo to expand from Morrigan's surface.

My heart and hopes fell when nothing seemed to happen. I was about to ask what happened when what looked like a physical sheet of energy and ice burst out from four points on the surface. And I was dropping to my knees when what felt like a psychic shockwave rippled past us, the magic felt alive and was both enraged and elated to be free to wreak havoc.

Rory caught me before I fell, blood streaming from my nose, ears, and eyes. I gasped as the wave dissipated. And just as she was asking if I was ok, Graz squeaked out, “Look!”

I nodded to my girl, and she helped me to the viewport, and we all just watched silently as in what seemed like painful slow motion, a slice of the asteroid, looking like some kind of massive flying saucer, just silently drifted up into the asteroid belt.

As Rory physically lifted me off my feet and sat me in one of the crew seats at a console to look me over, I whispered, “Wow.”

"Are you ok, Knith? You're bleeding!"

I patted her hand. "I'm fine." And I swayed, belying my words. "It was just a hell of a magic shockwave backlash. I think it was happy to be released to wreak havoc on Morrigan." I pointed out.

She narrowed her eyes then looked back to Mac, who shook his head once. "There was no backlash. The shockwave was contained and amplified to complete the first bisection."

"No, I mean after that. It hit like an incorporeal runaway trash hauler. I'll be fine for the next bisection." Then I looked over to Mac as Rory started cleaning the blood from my face. "Were we successful? Was it the mass we were expecting?"

He just looked at me, scrutinizing me as Aurora started probing me with her magic, like my word I was ok wasn't enough for her. Well, I guess I was overprotective of her too.

"The first bisection was successful, within point zero three percent of that projected by simulations." Mother answered for him.

Wow, that was...

"Hey!" I blurted when Rory shoved her icy magics into me. "A little warning, lady?"

She just said absently as I felt her magic spreading to every part of me, "There was no backlash, Knith. Every cell in your body has a residual magic burn. Not enough to do any permanent damage but..." She trailed off and grinned. "But it is already sloughing off of you, your partial magic immunity is amazing. So I remind you not to let it become common knowledge. There are some..."

She seemed to look for the proper words. “Fanatical magic factions on the world who would view that as a direct threat to their survival since magic is their only defense, and they may take... drastic measures.”

Then she cocked her head. “You always talk as if magic has intent or emotion. It is but a tool, it is not aware.”

I sighed, not this again. “I know what I experience, and know I'm not imagining things. It's like the artifact below decks, always whispering to us, calling us to come set it free or use it.”

Mac cocked a brow at that and moved over to us. “May I?”

I nodded hesitantly as he reached out. His eyes went cloudy white with electric blue lightning sparking deep inside. Then all of my exposed skin started to glow. I looked down at my hand in amazement as Rory traced fine silver lines on my skin that seemed to be rune circles rotating, Fae sigils and writing spinning around it all in exquisitely fine spellwork.

I whispered as I watched, mesmerized as it started to slowly fade. Mac swallowed and told Rory. “We must not speak of this to anyone, Daughter.”

She just nodded. Then she asked him like I wasn't even there, “There are two more bisections, they'll do the same, and she's only Human. Fragile.”

“Hello you two, what are you talking about? What did you do to my skin, Mac? What kind of Fae spellwork was written in the...”

Rory said quietly, “It was me. That isn't Fae spellwork. That is part of the writings on the artifacts of the Ka'Infinitum which pertains to life. I had encoded it into the Fae magic I infused in your genetic code to try to make the first Changeling.”

I swallowed. She had used some of the writings on the Forge of Creation in her attempts to help her race reproduce? Why was it on my skin when Mac did whatever he did so we could see it?

I voiced my questions, anxiety spiking, and Mac said, “I just revealed the magics you were rejecting, it was the magic of the artifact...” He narrowed his eyes in thought. “You say you can feel the intent of magic?”

I nodded. “It's more just impressions, but yes.”

“I believe the magic if it is somehow... aware, that it was just trying to get home. And part of you resonates like the artifacts. It is just conjecture, but whatever backlash there was that we could not see or feel like you, damaged you, trying to get into you like you were a vessel.”

Aurora pushed him away and said, “So sit still a moment while I address it.” Her icy magics slid into me again and I felt almost as if I were fizzing as every inch of me seemed to sizzle with that icy power. And... I felt better. I smiled at her and she smiled back.

Then I sighed and said, “Once we get readings on the cut, and any effect it had on the asteroid, we need to get to work on the next.”

She had concern and compassion in her lavender eyes as she whispered, “But we have to assume that each successive blast will have the same effect on you. Whatever phantom power, you are susceptible to may burn every cell like this each time, or worse.”

I shrugged. “This is the job. And besides, I have you to patch me back up again.” I stole a peck on her lips.

She sighed and smiled. “Again, you would not be my Knith Shade if you did not tilt at windmills.” She cupped my cheek and turned when her father spoke.

His tone was slow and warning when he told her, “She hears the calling of the artifact... no Human, let alone Fae can resist that call to power.”

“Titania's panties Papa, she's not going to go after the power for her own. This isn't Medieval Earth, and she's no power-mongering king, nor a Fae grasping beyond their reach. You, yourself, told me of their mental states... what the call does to them. Does Knith exhibit any of the signs? No. She's different, resistant, strong.”

Umm... “Uh, what are you two...”

“It's nothing. Father is being paranoid.” She assured me.

I sighed and said, “Then let's get back to work shall we?”

They both nodded as Beta closely watched us. Her eyes had been on Mac when he was intimating I could be corrupted. I think she was getting ready to intervene if he went beyond warning words. He'd disassemble her in a heartbeat, but she'd try. I loved me some Mother.

"And Mac? Fuck you. I'm not some power-mongering asswipe." I told him.

He gave me a crooked smirk and inclined his head in capitulation. "You are an enigma wrapped in a riddle, Knith Shade. And I find you endlessly interesting."

Just great. It was never good when the Greater Fae took interest in you.

And after a short rest and a slow flyby of the first cut, we were taking readings of the exposed materials that looked as if they had been sliced with a razor. Well, a razor that was about a million degrees as the newly exposed rock near the edges of the slice looked as if it had been melted, and the mineral and metal veins were fused into the stone.

The deeper portions of the cut, near the center of the slice, looked more cracked and torn, indicating that the plane of coherent magic hadn't penetrated as deeply as we had hoped, and it was the concussive force that was diverted inwardly along the plane had finished it, basically shattering the stone. There were deep cracks veining everywhere that made us a little nervous since our initial scans didn't map them before our cut.

We were getting detailed scans of the mineral, metal, and moisture content of the corkscrewing mass now at the bisection location, and they were extremely encouraging. Morrigan was the closest match we'd ever find to meeting the requirements of our growing fleet.

Shortly, I was out there again, trudging along as Mother blasted another Bangles song called 'Hazy Shade of Winter' as I fired anchor after anchor. I was about a mile from the first projector when I felt woozy for a moment, the asteroid and landscape seemed to sway, and I realized that it wasn't me, the Asteroid was rumbling under my feet.

One of the pointed arcs of stone silently cracked and tumbled in such slow motion, the microgravity and the centrifugal forces fighting each other, but the motion wasn't enough for the crumbling segment to reach the escape velocity from the mass of Morrigan. It looked to me like a giant who was laying down to slumber.

My helmet was displaying readings of the collapse. It would take almost five minutes at the rate it was moving. Rebound patterns were projected as Beta anticipated me, but none of the debris would endanger our det-cord.

"Are you guys reading this?" I asked thin air as Graz plastered herself to my visor to watch the event.

"There seems to be some settling and shifting of two dissimilar rocky surface plates along a ruptured fault line. Possibly a redistribution of material that was jarred by the bisection." Beta answered.

"A tectonic shifting. Like a very small scale earthquake." Aurora supplied.

“Ok, can someone tell the cute Fae princess to start speaking plain ship's Common? She's just stringing words together now.” I prompted.

Graz turned to me. “You don't know what an... oh... nevermind. I forget sometimes that you've been alive less than a Fairy fart.”

I rolled my eyes. “I get what Mother was saying, so I'm assuming Rory was just repeating it in brainy speak?” I had to smile at my girl's giggle over coms.

“On old Earth, the crust was made up of continental shelves, and when they rubbed up against each other and the pressure got too great it would cause tectonic shifts of those plates and it would cause upheavals that shook the earth as all that stored energy was released. Earthquakes.” Mac explained.

“Thank you, Mac. Now was that too hard for the rest of you?” I grinned and asked before any of the smartasses could retort as I stared off along the highlighted path in my vision. “It's not anything we need to worry about, is it? I mean, I know there is still settling in the Heart, especially since it is basically just a mostly empty honeycomb now. But they have all that safety tech to protect the miners and the active shafts there. We're just on the surface here so it shouldn't matter right? Unless one of those rock spire formations falls on our gear.”

“At this time, that is the only concern. We'll monitor them and reassess if they get more violent or may endanger the mission.” Beta said.

I nodded. “Alright then. Enough just standing around lollygagging, off I go.” And I started walking.

Mother shared as I made my way through the shadows of a tight corridor. “I've determined a more efficient use of our personnel. Since I do not require sleep, we can both lay det-cord in different directions tomorrow on the third and final cut, and meet in the middle. It would shave twelve hours off our time.”

I stopped. “Wait a second. Why weren't we doing this from the beginning? I thought you three were like, the brain trust or something. And I'm just out here wandering around in hard vacuum on the surface of an asteroid.”

Ok, I snorted when Beta offered with no apology in her tone. “Oops?”

Rory pacified me. “We had been staging things as if we were all biological people with the needs and limitations intrinsic to that. We had been so focused on the mission that we lost sight of all else. Then she echoed Mother, “Oops?”

Sighing I said in resignation as I shot another anchor, “I'll oops you when we get back home, lady.”

“Oh how exciting, it sounds like an amorous play being used as a punishment.”

“Keep it in your pants, Knith. I'm surprised all you Bigs even have the brainpower to breathe sometimes.” Graz told me.

“Nobody is asking you, you pint-sized terror.”

“That's why I'm offering my insight now. And hey, did you just call me little?” She buzzed her wings in threat. I smiled. Our little family was pretty amazing to me.

I had to steady myself on a rock outcropping when another... earthquake rumbled through my feet. “Ok everyone, enough chatter, I don't want to be out here a minute longer than I have to. This place is just shaking pretty good.”

I double-timed it.

CHAPTER 15

Collapse

As Rory and Oberon tended to me after the backlash from the second bisection had brought me to my knees, feeling as if I was on fire, Beta was taking readings from the new flat plane left from where we had carved yet another discus of material from Morrigan's surface.

She reported as they stemmed the bleeding from all my pores, a worried look in her eyes as she looked at me. “We were within three-tenths of a percent of our target de-massing. I'll line us up for the final cut. For the final cut. For the final... I'll line us....” She closed her eyes and her head shook for a moment. “Anomaly bypassed.”

Mac had moved so fast I hadn't seen him leave my side, as he moved her over, taking the controls as I looked at the pretty avatar with my own worry. She had lost more circuitry, she hadn't done that since the radiation belt. “Are you going to be ok, lady?” I asked.

She smirked. “Asks the Human bleeding from her eyes.”

“Smartass.” Then I looked sat my girl as she was wiping the blood of my newly healed skin, nudging my chin. “Can you...?”

She nodded, looking concerned for me as she went to check out Beta and run a systems scan on her. “I've got Mother, you go sleep to finish your recovery, Knith. These backlashes are taking an accumulative toll on you and I worry the next one may do something irreparable if you don't allow yourself time to recover."

A worried-looking Graz buzzed up to me, placing her hands on either side of my nose and searching my eyes. "Yeah, you don't look so hot."

"Fine. I'm heading to my rack, wake me when you have news about Mother's system health." I growled out.

They let me sleep four hours before waking me. Beta was as operational as could be expected, Rory shared that it wasn't affecting her much differently than the mission was affecting my body. We were both being stressed and taxed by the harsh environments we were being subjected to. Though she did worry about Beta since Mother has essentially been impervious to the effects of space that were doing a number to her avatar. The Leviathan was just that, a leviathan who was not swayed by the environment around her, a literal juggernaut in space. She wasn't used to being vulnerable, even if it was just by proxy.

"I know. I'll have a talk with her. I've got nothing else to do on my walk. I can't wait until this part is over and we can just move Morrigan onto an intercept heading. It was amazing and awe-inspiring for all of thirty minutes or so, but there is just so much rock you can look at without going mad." I said.

Graz chuckled as she buzzed up to sit on top of my head. "Heh, you want to tell her, or should I?"

Rory gave her a patient look and held her hand out palm up and the troublesome Sprite buzzed over to sit on it and my girl shared, “Well the final shear plane is only seventy percent cleared. Surface debris and regolith need to be moved so that the charges have surface contact.”

She showed her teeth in a cheesy smile as she gave apologetic jazz hands. I rolled my eyes and muttered, “Just space me now.”

She giggled. “That's the plan, my Knith. Let's, as you would say, get off this rock.”

I smirked as I shared, “I wouldn't say that.”

“But Beta shared you were thinking that at the end of your last extravehicular activity.”

I called out, “Mother! Stop listening in on my thoughts!”

I jumped a little when Mother's voice answered in my head, reminding me I was still in my armor. “Sorry, you just think too loud. Sometimes it is hard for the helmet to determine what is for me and what isn't.”

I pictured her biting the inside of her cheek like a mischievous imp. A habit Beta has been getting into. I wondered if it were possible for her avatars to develop their own personalities. I mean I know she varies them a little on purpose, but I really feel at times that being so far away from instant communications with her greater self, the Worldship, that Beta straying a little in her self image.

“I've been contemplating that question myself, especially when after data transfer delay contact, my primary processor seems a little frustrated with me. Her. Us. You know what I mean.”

So I asked point-blank. “Do your avatar bodies have enough computing power to store enough of you to be... well, a full person on their own without input from, well, you? This is so confusing.”

“I know that it is disconcerting that my emotional responses seem muted somehow, except anything intense. And I feel... fuzzy? Not having access to all my systems. I feel sort of alone.”

Nodding I shared out loud toward the internal cameras I knew Beta had hacked early on in the mission as I kissed the top of Rory's head and started to head out. “Again, welcome to the Human condition.”

Graz caught onto who and what I was talking about and she chirped out non-helpfully, “She's not Human, if anything, Beta is Mecha-Fae. Sexy tin can interface for the world.”

I reached up and mimed zipping her lips. She crossed her arms obstinately over her chest then pointed at the ceiling when Beta said, “Why thank you, Graz.”

“You two are certifiable.”

The Winter Maiden just laughed her silver chiming laugh as she trailed after me as we all went down to gear up. I just pointed at her and she snapped at my finger with her teeth, giving me a little wink. Mab's tits! I was going to go insane if we didn't get some alone time soon, but we had no privacy on the tug.

The only obstacle I wound up having to overcome was a fissure in the surface that was fifty feet across and almost a quarter-mile deep. It went on for thousands of feet in either direction so I walked back a few steps as Graz looked between the chasm and me and then pressed herself against my visor, looking out.

“Umm... Knith? Whatcha doing?”

I started running increasing the downward thrust of my suit, it really took some muscle to accelerate all the mass on my back, but I didn't need much momentum.

“Knith? Have you gone space happy? That's at least fifty feet across, you mental Big! Ahhhhhhhhhh!”

I leapt and shut off my suit thrusters as I got concerned calls from Beta, Aurora, and Mac who were watching the feeds from my suit.

With a smirk, I informed the unruly lot, “Micro-gravity.”

Then I went pale, whoops. I was gaining altitude fast. My armor was calculating my apogee to be about a mile up in about nine minutes and a half orbit before the gravity of the asteroid pulled me down. And the impact, even at negligible Gs, with the mass of the det-cord spool on my back, would be more than my armor could handle.

As everyone was yelling out things to me in overlapping voices that became a cacophony of sound I couldn't pick out the individual words from, I put my lower lip under my teeth and whistled shrilly.

They all silenced except the screaming Graz. “Everyone just shut your pie-holes and let me handle this.”

I fired the micro thrusters in the suit to cancel my ascent, and then throttled them up and then winced at myself for not letting the autonomous systems handle it. “Ow,” I said in anticipation as we shot toward the rocky landscape below as we reached the other side.

Aurora was asking as Graz screamed again, “Ow? What is it? Are you still...” She stopped talking as we slammed into one of those rock formations, snapping the rib-like stone arch and then tumbled into another before hitting and skipping along the ground until the suit took over and arrested my mistake.

I hopped up onto my feet again and said, “I'm ok!”

The love of my life just sighed out. “You're an idiot.”

“Ow.”

So on the third leg of the final cut is where things started to get... interesting. I was having to woman handle rocks and debris out of the way, to get down to the bedrock I could fire anchors into. I even had a skin jockey plasma scraper that was blowing aside or vaporizing the loose, gritty regolith.

Every muscle was going to ache for days after this, but I was determined to get it done, so I soldiered on. Knowing that since Beta was on the same hemisphere, moving to the projector from the other side, that this would all be over soon and I could go die from boredom as we pushed this rock into place and we rejoined our fleet. Nirvana.

Beta was playing ‘Renegade’, by a band called Styx in my helmet as I approached a gap between some unusually large rock formations. I looked through as I sliced a boulder the size of my Tac-Bike to push aside before clearing some regolith down to the bedrock with the scraper that was struggling to keep up as its over-taxed power source was starting to give out. They were never designed for continuous use like this.

I could see the final last projector just a couple hundred yards away, and Beta was already there, waving to me and signaling my visor to zoom in so I could see her little smirk. Of course, she beat me. I sighed and felt... Human.

The New Hope would arrive as I got there, as they were currently finishing up diverting a half-mile wide asteroid that was approaching uncomfortably close and might stray into our escape lane.

“Yuck it up buttercup. I'll see you in about twenty minutes. I've got a bit of rubble to move.” I said.

The smug AI said, “What? I didn't say anything, Knith. I've just been hanging out here, looking at the stars, for the last ten minutes or so.”

“She doesn't sound sincere, does she?” Graz said.

“Not a bit.”

Ok, I grinned at the pleased noise the surly AI made.

I sighed, cranked the music, then trudged on, clearing the way and silently thanking the fates that we didn't have to clear the path this entire time. This was getting really old and I was glad to be on the home stretch.

It was a tight squeeze between the rock formations that looked like two giant fangs raising out of the asteroid. As I struggled I looked back attempting to gauge how much my path would be diverted if I went around the base of them. "Mother?"

Beta said, "It would be outside the acceptable variance of the shear plane if you did so, and this is the most critical cut. Sooo... you'll have to make your way through. I bet you're questioning that extra nutrition bar before you left."

I blinked at her playfulness. "Is it dump on Humans day or something?"

Then Graz, Beta, and even Rory and Mac on the coms said together, "Every day is dump on Humans day."

I chuckled at the ages-old joke. "No respect, I tell ya." Then I sighed and started pushing my way through the narrow passage, the spool on my back scraping the stone in places it was so tight. There was more room near my feet so I hefted the spool off and rolled it in front of me and it sort of half floated as it unspooled slowly, its mass helping to string out the det-cord until it was past the gap and sort of started twisting slowly above the surface.

I was grinning when I saw the gap widening in just a few more steps, and the rest of the way was already cleared... had Beta been here longer than she said? I was just glad it was finally all over.

Beta was making her way toward me to retrieve the spool when the world started swaying again.

The vibrations in my feet had groaned and creaking translating into the atmosphere of the suit. The shaking got violent and then with a loud crack, the passage started getting narrower, I started moving faster, placing my hands on either side of the opening, feeling the walls starting to lean in toward each other as the ground started falling away slowly.

"Go faster Knith!" Graz was screeching.

Mother started taking leaping bounding steps toward us as I was calling out, "I'm going, I'm..." The two masses moving toward each other would take a ton of energy to slow, something I didn't have.

My shoulders were scraping the sides and I had to turn sideways. I saw the horror on Beta's face as she was still twenty or thirty yards away, arm outstretched as we exchanged looks, knowing I wouldn't make it.

No, I wasn't giving up. As long as I was alive I was going to fight, I pulled up the scraper on its lanyard and jammed it between the arced pillars as their sweeping points hit each other, reducing the tips to drifting rubble as I heard the cracks and grinding in the suit, slowing the collapse. The scraper was nothing to the mass in motion as it started crushing fast. I thought fast as my armor started crushing, and re-configuring itself to reinforce the crushing zones.

I couldn't breathe as I felt my ribs compressing and one snap. My helmet started to crush and Graz was screaming in pain as she was pressed between my skull and the visor. In a panic, hearing Beta screaming my name, I took everything I knew about surviving a vacuum, I sent a last-second command to my armor and the nano-panels flowed off of my arms and abdomen to form a solid plate of carbon-reinforced armor between the two columns of stone.

I could feel the sweat boiling away on the portions of my skin exposed to space. My skull hurt it was pressed so tightly in this rock crusher hell I found myself in. Panic had me hyperventilating and the freezing chill of space on parts of my body was threatening to send me into hypothermic shock. This was it, there was nothing else I could do, and I wouldn't even die on the world I loved.

My vision was dimming as my body tried to deal with the excruciating pain by shutting down, but I struggled to remain conscious as I heard the plate cracking and groaning on the verge of failure. I slurred out on coms, "Aurora... I... Rory... sorry... I..."

Then with a bellowing scream of effort, Beta was on the coms and the pressure seemed to give, ever so slightly, allowing blood to flow more freely. I heard the groaning of stone and I blinked, seeing Beta's face a couple of feet from mine, where the gap was wider.

I kept blinking as my senses returned. Beta was there, her back to one pillar, her arms pushing against the other as she almost roared out, "Knith! Drop down to the surface, there's more of a gap there. Hurry, my systems are..."

There was a groan in my suit and I saw one of her arms start to compress, sparks drizzling. I tried to move down but the helmet and chest plate were jammed on the rocks. I rasped out, “Graz? Graz are you ok? I've got to drop the helmet for a moment. Don't hold your breath.”

Beta was screaming a challenge as her arms crushed more. I exhaled all the air I could, closed my eyes, then signaled the suit. The helmet bled away into nano-panels as did the chest plate and I scrabbled downwards, my gauntlets gaining purchase even though my arms felt frozen from the exposure already, but the skin is a good seal to vacuum believe it or not.

I was panicking needing to breathe and could feel the moisture boiling away from my tightly closed eyes and my face. And... I was free. With a thought, all my armor flowed back over my body, sealing, showing systems and integrity at sixty percent nominal, with alarms and warnings and flashing lights everywhere in my vision.

Then I crawled and scrabbled for my life. Through the gap, over Beta's feet. And just as I pulled my feet clear, there was a horrific crunching sound over coms and Beta made a distressed sound. I was barely aware of Mac and Rory almost yelling over the coms to us to report, but all I could see, all I could hear when I opened my eyes and gasped in the air to my lungs, was Beta, as the pillars continued on their inexorable course, her crushed arms were useless and her torso was crushing slowly as she looked at me with hope.

“Knith? Are you... Knith... are... ok... you... Knith ok.” Sparks started drizzling from ruptures in her subframe as I struggled to my feet to move toward her.

My voice was a harsh rasp, “I'm ok. Beta. You saved me.”

“G... ggg... good.” Then her eyes widened as she looked at me, and I felt a pang of guilt like I never have in all my years as she whispered, sounding so very small, “I don't... don't... want to die.”

I wanted to go to her as her body was compressed even more and her head started to crumple. I whispered, “This is your avatar... you're still with us.”

She said, “Not my... not Knith... my last... hours... four... I.” Then with a silent crunch, I could feel in my feet as her coms gave out, the fucking nightmare of an asteroid took her from us as the pillars came to a rest against each other like she hadn't meant a thing to it.

I dropped to my knees and said to the two voices yelling at me to report as I gave a hoarse whisper, “She's gone.” Beta, who was sort of becoming her own person outside of her main databanks of the Worldship, her last four hours of experiences lost forever. And she had been afraid.

I just screamed at how unfair the universe was, and I was more sure than ever that all the races had it wrong. If there were gods, then how could they let that happen, how could they let any of this happen?

I heard moaning in my helmet near my ear which had me quieting, standing again, cradling my ribs which my armor's health sensors were reporting were cracked. “Graz?” No response. I looked at the only interior camera view that was operational. Graz was tangled in my hair, unmoving, one leg at an unnatural angle and her wings were completely shredded.

This knocked me out of the spiral of pain, regret, guilt, and sorrow. I responded to the two Greater Fae finally, “Get down here now! We lost Beta, and Graz looks in bad shape. I think she's dying!”

“Almost there now! Your vitals are erratic, what happened down there?” Mac was already calling out.

I spat out with raw hate in my tone, “Morrigan is trying to kill us all!”

CHAPTER 16

Special Hell

On the New Hope a few minutes later, Aurora was frantically pouring huge amounts of magic into a still Graz. I had slapped away Oberon when he offered to heal my injuries and the cold burns on my skin as I hissed at him. “Get Beta, we're not leaving her here.”

He had started, “It's just a machine, Kni...”

“Do you really fucking believe that?” I was in his face in challenge.

Not my smartest move since he could tear me apart with a pinky finger, but he backed down, holding his hands out in placation. “I'll retrieve her now.” And he left us. I didn't want to know how he was going to do so, since we didn't have an EVA suit for him, but I saw him walk on the skin of the Leviathan without a suit before... while he was shooting lightning from his hands.

Aurora looked pale, even for her porcelain white complexion, as she gasped and stopped what she was doing. I looked on to see what looked like a glowing cocoon of silky white magic where Graz had been.

I winced as I reached out to steady my girl as she told me, “She's alive. Barely. She's in her chrysalis now. This normally happens much further on in a Sprite's lifetime, but I had to put so much healing power into her it has already begun. She'll be in a sort of stasis for weeks, and will come out... changed."

Changed?

She caught me when I swayed, and I flinched away from her ice cold touch that burned my damaged skin. "Now lay down! I need to see to your injuries. I can't do much, I used so much for Graz and I need to preserve most of what I have left for the final bisection. But your ribs, your skin, need attention now."

I couldn't argue with her when she was in her avenging angel mode. And I had no fight left in me. I laid down, Beta on my mind. I whispered, "She sacrificed herself for me."

She nodded sadly and I gasped when her icy magics pushed inside me as soon as I was laying down. And the love of my life started healing me from within.

The princess of both the Un-Seelie Court and my heart finished as we heard the echos of the airlock cycling for the first time. The chronometer in my suit was blurring and pulsating, but I was shocked to see that an hour had gone by as the worst of my injuries, which were more extensive than we originally thought, were healed.

I swung my legs and hopped off the table and started to sway as my legs almost buckled before my armor took over mobility for me, moving my legs for me. Rory had grasped at me but I told her, "I'm fine," as I jogged toward the ladders down, grabbing the rails loosely and just sliding down with my feet at the side of the rails.

She called out to me in frustration and concern, “No! You are most certainly not fine. Any other human would be flat on their back right now, there is still a lot of damage to address later. Get your stubborn, Human-y ass back here!”

I had to chuckle, pushing all the poisonous emotions I was sauteing in to the back of my mind, not dwelling on things, I called up as I started sliding down to the next level as she just thudded to the deck after just jumping down. She sounded like a solid iron ingot landing, but making it look as if she had simply hopped down a single step. She may have bent the old alloy deck-plate a little. “Human-y? Seriously? I thought the Greater Fae were supposed to be well educated.”

She started to say as she caught up with me just as I entered the maintenance bay, “I may have picked up a thing or... two... from...”

I finished her thought for her in my own head, “Graz.”

We reached the airlock just as the final green light lit on the panel on the door, indicating that the pressure had equalized and I slammed my palm on the big red button to cycle the inner door open.

Rory and I both stood there, our mouths agape at the sight of Oberon, King of Faerie, standing there with the remains of our friend, almost crushed beyond recognition, circuits and servos hanging out all over from the splintered shell that was as tough and durable as the most magi-tech battle hardened armor plating used in the Ready Squadron.

In his other hand, he held a mostly empty det-cord spool in full gravity like it was inconsequential even though it had to weigh at least four hundred pounds empty. He dropped it, then this seemingly unstoppable titan did the last thing I would have imagined after seeing him looking so majestic and triumphant. He dropped to one knee, eyes wide, then gasped, inhaling greedily.

He bled back into his middle aged Human guise as he panted and gasped out, “It's hard to remember how to breathe again after being out there for a bit.” He smirked at us as Rory ran to his side to support him by his shoulders, causing me to cock a brow.

Before we left, she wouldn't have shown any concern for the man at all, and certainly wouldn't be helping him with worry creasing her brow. Maybe there was hope for them after all? Then again, they did have literally forever to reconcile, so I guess it was inevitable at some time.

Then his face got serious as he looked down at his precious cargo, and he cradled it in both arms as he told me while Rory wiped frost off of his skin, “I may have done more damage, busting her out of the rocks. This is all that was left of her.”

I nodded and moved up to take her from him. I didn't expect them to understand, but I have known the real Mother longer than them. She was my friend, my family, my confidant for years before I met either of them. And Beta... well I didn't fully understand her or what she was becoming, but she was part of Mother, so I loved her. And now she was gone and we'd never know what she was capable of becoming as she seemed to be evolving before our eyes. And even not having Mother's full AI onboard, she had been afraid to die, and yet she still sacrificed herself for me.

I turned from them as they both watched me intently, heads cocking in the same manner hands clasping in a nervous habit. They were more alike than either of them could see. I kicked over a stowage box, the gear falling out across the deck-plates. Then with my foot I uprighted it again and lowered the remains of my friend into it and then sealed it.

Then I looked at them as I slid it into the cargo racks and initiated mag-lock on it to secure it safely. I exhaled shakily and Rory was there, holding one of my hands between hers as she sought out my eyes with hers. “She was very brave and noble. We'll get her back home.”

I looked between her and the box, then I... as Graz would have put it, 'Knithed out', and said, “I feel like we should say something.”

We turned as Mac started talking in a low, respectful tone, “Many Fae wonder why I have taken such a liking to the upstart race of Humans. It is because they know a truth we cannot conceive, and can see what we have never known, how fleeting life is and the gift it is to all of us. And they have words for times such as this, when one of their own is taken before their brief flare of life had burned out naturally.”

“My comfort will come from the sea. The stillness of calm waves will gently drift by. I will be as one with the sea. When the sun sets on the ocean blue, remember me as I will always remember you. As the sun rises... go live life as full as can be. Apart... you and me... but be at peace for I am free."

I heard a pinging tinkle on the deck, and saw a diamond-like crystal starting to melt. I looked up to see Aurora to see another tear fall from her cheek. I pulled her to me and hugged her as I said, "Let's get this gods be damned mission over with, I'm so done with this fucking asteroid."

She smiled sadly and nodded once and we turned to Mac as he said, "I secured the last of the det-cord run and made the connection to the projector."

Morrigan rumbled and shook causing the superstructure of the Tug to groan and shake in protest.

I growled out as we all headed up to the bridge, "That's it you bitch, complain all you want. Our people need you so you're coming with us."

Mac deftly took the controls and we smoothly gained altitude, backing off as he orbited the massive astral body to hover a few miles off from the surface near the primary projector. He asked, "Rory? Do you have enough power? We can wait for you to rest up and recover your..."

I was sort of proud when she cut him off, sounding a heck of a lot like me being stubborn whenever I over-taxed myself, "I'm fine. Let us do what my Knith Shade says, and get this over with. I am so over this little field trip myself."

We all stood by the forward window, looking down. Mac looked at Rory, worry in his eyes then I could taste the power they were pulling to themselves. And just like the other times, I could feel it mixing. Mac blew a note on the harmonica and I could feel the amplification and the power from the artifact below decks feeding it as the signal was sent. The det-cord went off, hundreds of little explosions.

Then everything went wrong. The planes of force bloomed and pulsed, and Rory staggered. I grabbed her as she slumped and braced myself for the backlash only I could feel. But the discus of Morrigan's surface seemed to crumble before my eyes, as a violent explosion seemed to shatter it, sending billions of tons of debris flying at us.

I was starting to call out to Mac as collision alert alarms started blaring, but the magic backlash tore into me, scouring me, burning me. I barely clung to consciousness as I saw Mac explode into his Fae form and slashed a hand while holding one up toward the window. As a shield bloomed in front of us, a section of rock the size of the New Hope herself, was struck by another wall of force, crumbling it.

But unlike Aurora, who had time to form her shield properly and anchor it to other sources of mass, physics kicked in. Even magic had to follow the laws of physics for the most part. And the tug was thrown to the side when Oberon went flying to the far bulkhead, denting it deeply.

I fell, cradling Rory as we tumbled along the deck until whatever spell they used for gravity gave way and we were tumbling through the air. Even though he tried to keep his focus on the other shield as he struggled up, there was too much coming at us. We were pummeled by shards of Morrigan from pebble sized to rocks that were dozens of meters across.

The incredibly tough and durable tug took the beating while damage klaxons went off, and decompression alarms. Emergency systems status data was scrolling in my visor. And then... it was over. I hit the bulkhead hard as I was shutting off all the audible alarms. And, besides the sound of air being vented somewhere in the ship, there was silence.

I hit the deck hard when Mac ran to the controls, gravity reasserting itself. Then I laid Rory down and stood to run to another station. Mac was skillfully flying us to a safe distance, away from the expanding cloud of debris behind us that was wreaking havoc on the asteroid field now.

Looking over first the critical systems, and seeing blast doors had lowered to contain the hull breech, then the reactors to make sure they weren't in danger of going critical or anything, I reviewed the data to see just what the hells had just happened.

I whispered, “Mother Fairy humper.”

Mac was calling out as he fought the controls as damage to some of the maneuvering thrusters was displayed on the main screen, “What was that?”

I shook my head as I looked at the scans. “There was a void, like a blister under the surface that the sensors had mapped out as a massive cavern system. It was gasses from organic molecules, likely a huge methane pocket from decomposing granite from whatever planetary body this asteroid had come from. It ignited when the bisection was made. It was the equivalent of one megaton. It's started Morrigan rotating on all three axis' now.”

He growled out. “I think you're right. Morrigan is trying her damnedest to kill us all. This is some sort of special Hell we're in.”

I nodded and swayed, all the damage from the magic backlash was multiplied by the prior injuries I had and the new ones from hitting the bulkhead. I swallowed, “Are we in a safe place? I don't know how much longer I can stand.”

Aurora moaned and started blinking, before sitting up. She looked around to see all the warning lights and damaged systems scrolling on the screens. “What's going on? What... Knith!”

I took a step toward her and collapsed. She caught me before my helmet hit the floor. I smiled in apology, “Things sort of went FUBAR while you were out, love.”

She asked, her eyes darting around the controls, “What's FUBAR?”

Mac was chuckling out, “Fucked up beyond all...” And I was out.

CHAPTER 17

Let It Be

We had heard back from home by the time Mac, who wasn't a very talented healer, had me in any shape to be moving around. He had forcefully told Rory that she had overextended already, that she needed to rest and recover some strength before she did permanent damage to herself. I concurred.

She had just looked at me, “Only if you rest too. We've a window before we hear back from the Leviathan how we are to proceed.”

I was about to argue when Mac grunted and growled, “She's right, neither of you are any good to us in the shape you're in. I've got to inventory the damage, and inspect the ship to make sure it is still capable of pushing this rock. I've only gone half way through the damage reports.”

Sighing I muttered, “Fine.”

That would be right about where Mother or Graz would say something sarcastic in my helmet, but instead there was silence for the first time since... well since the Brigade Enforcer Academy. And it almost feels like Graz has been in my ear just as long.

I sighed out as I grabbed my Sprite friend's cocoon from where it was strapped in the co-pilot's seat and Rory led me to where the berths were. I started to ask on reflex, "Mother, can you play..." I trailed off then manually pulled up my play list on random shuffle.

A retrospective piece called Let it Be, by a band called the Beatles started and I cursed silently, the universe can be a cruel mistress at times, since this would be exactly what Mother would have played for me at that time.

We just lay there, Aurora curled into a ball, holding Graz as I wrapped around her. I just watched all the data scrolling in my peripheral vision, staring at the numbers on one damaged system which Mac hadn't stumbled upon yet, while Rory's breathing slowed as she slipped into a fitful sleep. When the music stopped, in the sound dampened room, I swear I could hear my armor's auto repair systems working, burning off the emergency magi-tech packs, as the armor integrity slowly, painfully ticked up.

If I thought my girl's sleep was fitful, mine bordered on nightmarish, and all the while, the artifact down in the vault was whispering into my head, telling me to use it, that it could fix everything if I just let the power free. I woke with a start, not knowing if it had been a bad dream or if the Fairy humping thing was trying to worm its way into my subconscious.

I knew how powerful the Forge of Creation was, since it birthed our infinite universe, our reality. But in doing so, it had shattered itself. I absently wondered if the artifacts in the Ka'Ifinitum were all the pieces of the source of all magic, the source of life, the source of... nightmares, or if they were just the tiny shards of it that the Fae had found, or were birthed from since they are magic incarnate. Are they just an expression of its inner self, a way to interact with the other life it had created?

Was the magic so broken, like the Forge, that just this tiny bit, though impossibly huge to someone like me who could not wield power like that, was still barely able to keep our world alive, powering her through the stars to our destination.

If so the Forge, which produced the Big Bang, was infinitesimally small. All the artifacts I saw when I witnessed them myself, would barely fit in a footlocker. I'd have to ask about it sometime. Is it possible there are other shards of the Forge scattered through the cosmos?

I had so many questions that likely had no answers, at least not any I could comprehend. And I looked at the damage report again, at a number that was worrisome. Maybe I'd never get those answers after all. The chrono started chiming and I shook Rory gently, leaning down to kiss her sublime, graceful neck. “Come on lady, time to get up. We should be hearing from the Worldship in a few minutes.”

She stretched like a feline from her head to her toes and purred out, “Don't start something we don't have time to finish, my Knith.”

She slid gracefully off the rack to her feet, and I, out of habit, straightened up the cot and remade the covers, tucking Graz's cocoon securely under them. We stopped by the mess on the way back to the cockpit to grab something to eat and drink, and brought some up to Mac.

The moment we stepped onto the deck, his eyes narrowed at me as he complimented Rory for her selection of food since he'd never make the mistake of thanking her. He just watched me as I made my way to my station to check on our status. He just kept watching. I noted one of the screens behind him. Damage reports. Fuck me sideways, he saw. I just shook my head. I knew there was a solution, we didn't need to worry Aurora just now. Focus on one problem at a time.

He huffed and then said instead, “Both of you look much better. I can see you are almost up to full strength now that your magic has restored itself, Aurora.”

She nodded, “Yes Papa. I'll need to take some time to work more on Knith today, but her natural healing has got a head start on it.”

I rolled my shoulders. She was right, there were still some aches and pains, and one of my ribs still twinged when I stretched, but left to my own devices, I'd be good as new in a day or three.

He looked to be studying me. “Yes, Mir tells me that healing is just one of our Knith's extraordinary gifts for a Human, speed, strength, healing. And I can detect nothing but pure Human life energy coming off of her. Does she have any other... abnormalities? You did a superb job in sequencing her genes from what I have been able to piece together. This alone can't be why both the Queens of the divided courts have taken an interest in her."

I flipped the man off. "I'm right here. There's no call to be talking about me like I'm not here, you old fart."

He chuckled, "And so you are my dear Shade."

Aurora looked agitated. I assumed her father knew all there was to know about me, especially since he has been helping me from the moment I met him, and has been an ally and friend. Then again, Greater Fae are all about outmaneuvering people to deceive them in the most creative of ways. Is that why he took an interest in me, because the Winter then the Summer Queen had?

I'm sure there was some of that in it, but I think I'm a curiosity to him, and he is acting as if he knows all so that secrets may slip. That and I really do believe we're friends. Sure our friendship is strained while my girlfriend believes he is a child abandoning ass, but we have a friendship based on mutual respect... and impeccable taste in music.

Ok, he was smirking just then, like he knew what was going through my head. Then he just told her, "Well I approve. Though she's got more courage than sense at times. I was there when she was charging ships on the skin. Who does that?"

I pointed out, "Still here. And if I remember right, you were doing the same thing. Mab's tits man."

He bowed graciously, “Touche. Though I'm a little more durable than you, no matter how good of job my daughter did in creating an evolved Human.”

Before Rory could say anything, her eyes narrowed in suspicion, an incoming signal was pinging the comms console. We all moved around it and saw it contained no data packets, no video, just a simple message from President Yang herself.

It read, “All of our engineers and astrophysicists have analyzed the spin of Morrigan after the blowout incident. They all concur that the New Hope doesn't have the fuel to arrest the spin on two of the axis before you can start moving the mass onto the intercept vector. The Morrigan mission is scrubbed. You are to proceed with targets Beta and Gamma instead. That will give us time for the secondary contingency at the next asteroid belt. Your efforts have been valiant, and your contributions have been noted. Proceed with the alternate plan and we'll see you on the world in a few weeks.”

Then it was quantum encoded with her identification codes.

We looked at each other. They'd given up on our goal, and already viewed it as a failure, and were just ready to limp along with the less palatable solution because it was... easier?

Mac muttered to us, “Well that's a fine how do you do. They've given up. What say you two? Do we go for second prize?”

I growled, feeling a seething anger bubbling up in me, “Fuck that! This rock killed Beta, and almost killed Graz. She's beat our ship to hells, but now it's our turn.”

Princess Aurora of the Un-Seelie Winter Court, the Winter Maiden herself, stood tall and regal and proclaimed, "Yeah, what the brash one said," as she smirked and winged a thumb my way. My grin was so big my cheeks ached at her playfulness in the face of adversity.

Mac scrubbed his chin and said, "Right then, if we're to properly ignore our orders, then we just have to figure out how to stop this top from spinning."

We sat down and started crunching numbers. We kept hitting two different walls. With everything we proposed, we either ran out of time, or fuel... or both. If we didn't use fuel to slow the rotation to a stop, instead used Mac and Rory to slow the mass down, we'd need about six years. The Leviathan would overshoot us by then and we'd never be able to accelerate the Morrigan enough to rendezvous from behind, unless we had the fuel to burn for about eight hundred years.

If we used the fuel up stopping the mass rotation, then we'd need to use Rory and Mac's magic to accelerate the ship and the asteroid. Missing the rendezvous again.

Trying to think outside the box I prompted, "We're only looking at the resources we have available to us in the New Hope. Can we utilize the resources of Morrigan or the asteroid field to our advantage in some way?"

Rory tapped her chin, while Mac ran more numbers. Then she said, "We know there are fissionable materials, and we unfortunately know there are organic molecules. Besides that, there isn't anything that the asteroids can offer us in this instance, unless they have another Tug hiding behind a rock out there."

Not for the first time, I regretted that we took only one vessel. But the logistics and the backup plans in case we failed precluded us using both. I prompted, "Well what about the artifact? Can it be used in concert with the Focus to arrest the spin?"

He said as Rory looked deep in thought, "You know and have seen our limitations when dealing with magic in a zero gravity vacuum. We would need to generate enough energy to counteract the energy of the spinning mass. And the numbers for a seven mile wide asteroid are staggering, all that motion is a mind boggling amount of inertial energy."

"And we'd need something to push against of equal or more power. We have one of the smallest artifacts with us, so it would take a long time for it's smaller... well we'll say mass value of its power, pushing against it to make a difference. True it would be many times quicker than if we did it with our own power, but we're still talking weeks and we'd miss out acceleration envelope."

My slow mind churned and pointed out that he equated mass to power and inertia to power. Something in the back of my head was telling me that that was important. I wished Mother were here, she'd be able to tell me why it was important. She always knew what I was thinking better than I did. Then my eyes widened when I realized what it was. I blurted, "Then we have all that we need!

There are two resources we didn't list in the asteroid belt, and there's an almost endless amount of both."

I pointed at the cloud of rocks in space around us. "What do you see?"

Aurora stepped closer to the window, one brow cocked as she looked between me and the rocks that went on for a million miles or more.

Mac wasn't in a guessing mood as he warned me, "Knith?"

Then Rory started to laugh. She waved a hand at the expanse of asteroids and chirped out as she chuckled, "It was right there before us and we were blind to it. Don't you see Papa? She's right."

He growled at her, "Don't make me pull this space ship over, what did we miss?"

I said, "Mass, inertial energy, a boundless supply of it."

The man's eyes clouded over in white as he turned to the window and joined his daughter. Then he slowly started nodding and chuckling himself as he mused, "You may be right. We just may be able to pull this off." Then he smirked at us and teased me, "You do know that if it works, they're going to name this the Shade Maneuver, don't you?"

I muttered, "Space me now."

They could use their combined magics with the artifact, coupled with the harmonica Focus to push against the endless mass of the entire asteroid belt, and harvest all the momentum and inertia in all the stones to help push against the rotation of the largest object inside that same field. All the brainacs back home hadn't taken the debris field itself into consideration when they ran all their simulations.

I grinned like a maniac as I whispered, “We're coming for you you lifeless hunk of stone,” and we started to plan.

CHAPTER 18

Move You Bitch!

That's how we wound up laying Mac down in a rack to rest five hours later. He looked beyond exhausted, his face still straining. He was so weak he couldn't maintain his Human glamour. But we were all grinning like predators. Morrigan never saw us coming, but now she gently rotated on a single axis, the space around us was completely clear for thousands of miles.

He said as his eyes started to close as soon as he laid down, “Four hours, no more. We're cutting it all too close as it is if we want to have any safety margin.”

“Yes Papa.”

I echoed her with a toothy grin, “Yes Papa.”

He muttered with a grin as he drifted off, “Why my baby girl chose a smartass like you, I'll never know.”

She giggled and I spun on her, “What are you laughing about, woman? Get in bed, now. You've over extended again. I'll watch over that floating mass of bad tempered stone below while you two recharge.”

I gave her a peck on the lips as I led her to her berth and placed the cocoon in her hands and sat there until she closed her eyes and drifted off. Then I sighed and headed for the environmental control deck instead of the bridge, to look at the biggest problem we had.

There had to be something that could be done down here. I grabbed a scanner and a tool kit and went to work.

As I rooted out the problem with the systems, I thought about the display of power I had witnessed from Oberon and Aurora. This mission has taxed their abilities over and over, yet when they needed to weave the most powerful casting of magic I have ever witnessed before, they showed just how formidable the Greater Fae were as a species.

Humans have been lead to believe that the whole reason the Fae and other magical races had hidden from us until we were starting to plan for the Worldship, hoping our lacking technology would be up to the task by the time of Leviathan's completion, was because we had greater numbers.

We... were so wrong. I have witnessed only two Fae, with the tools they had available to them to boost their power, take herculean slices out of a mini moon. And if that wasn't frightening enough, then watching what they had completed just a few minutes ago, showed me that no matter our numbers or technology... mankind had absolutely no chance of ever winning a war against them.

The only thing holding them back... was themselves. The two things about their own culture were the only things keeping them from wiping the Human plague off the Earth long before we went to space together. Firstly, the divided courts would never work together just on principal, unless it meant saving their entire race, like was necessitated by the expansion of the sun, Sol.

And second, they were too used to being eternal, and death is such a foreign concept to them that it is shocking and paradigm shifting to them when it occurs. And they knew if they raged war against the humans, they would surely win, quite handily, but a few billion annoyances with weapons were sure to get lucky and overwhelm a few of them before the Human race was eradicated, and any losses of Greater Fae life was unacceptable to them... so they hid their presence from us.

I felt sort of inconsequential as I monitored the ship's position and the rotation of Morrigan as they wove their magic in a silver sphere that stretched for hundreds of miles in all directions, intricate glowing sigils and Fae script tied all the asteroids inside of the mammoth construct together, whether hundreds of yards across to single grains of sand as they drifted toward their ultimate destruction a million years distant at the black hole that pulled at them.

To me, it felt as if my soul was vibrating inside of me as the magic seemed to take on a life of its own when they drew from the artifact, and amplified their combined magics to push the sphere outward even farther, causing static to arc from the little hairs on the back of my neck and along my arms.

When the time came, they knew instinctively, their magics in sync, and they both thrust their arms forward and pushed. I had been forced to my knees by the force of the magic that rushed out toward Morrigan.

Though there is no sound in space, I got the feeling that the asteroid was bucking and fighting against the grip of some invisible magic hand at a scale that was too great for my mind to fully grasp. The New Hope shuddered, her superstructure groaning.

Then it started to happen. The rotation velocities started changing as Oberon and Rory strained, gasping and actually sweating. The asteroids in the debris field at first, stated to slowly move away from us, then started to gain momentum, and before long they were hurtled away at unimaginable speeds. It was like a wave went out from the ship in all directions, and it wiped away anything in its path as the kinetic energy was removed from Morrigan and moved to them as they used the asteroids as an anchor to push back at the small moon.

The sensors followed that wave as it rippled away, first a hundred then two hundred miles, then five hundred and by the time it had grown to a thousand miles from us in the epicenter, I had realized that hours had passed and Oberon caught Aurora as she dropped to a knee, gasping as their magic faded.

I was blinking in awe at them, then looked at the readings and sputtered, “Zero, zero, zero. The rotation on all three axis of Morrigan has been canceled out! By the gods, you did it!” We only needed two axis rotations to be neutralized, and I was so mesmerized watching them that I hadn't notice when they had accomplished that and now the only inertial energy left in the asteroid was its momentum along its flight path.

Aurora had just shrugged and looked at me and said while she regained her feet, “Eh, I wasn't doing anything else at the moment, so...?”

I smirked at her, even though she and her father sort of intimidated and scared me at that moment. Right up until the man just fell forward, just to be caught an inch before his face hit the deck. As impressive a feat of strength that was from my diminutive ice princess, she still struggled slightly as she pulled him to standing and supported him by moving under his arm.

She had told me, “He moved most of the magic, from the artifact himself. The fool of an old man. 'Oooo look at me, I'm the king of the Fae, I'll do most of the work, you just aim it daughter.' Idiot.”

Grinning and helping her with Oberon I said apologetically, “My sarcasm is wearing off on you. It's a good look. Now lets get you two to the racks, and I'll look at our status while you rest.”

She shook her head, “I'll join you after we get Papa situated.”

I wiggled my fingers in the air. “Ooo look at me, I'm the hottest Fae Princess ever. I've overextended my powers too, but I'll act all tough for the sexiest Enforcer ever.”

This made her snort and deflate, shedding her air of power to show her exhaustion. “Point taken my Knith Shade. I'm the hottest am I? And who is this sexy Enforcer you...”

I blew a raspberry at her to shut her up. I got a tired giggle in response.

Now here I was, working on the problem that was going to be our biggest obstacle yet if we didn't get it all sorted out. After what I saw, I had no doubt we'd be able to get Morrigan moved onto the correct course and speed for the Leviathan to overtake and capture her, so that wasn't my worry.

When we got a reprimand from the President as I was working, telling us to abandon our current course of action and were re-ordered to proceed to targets beta and gamma, I had just snorted and recorded a message and sent it out on a data burst. "With all due respect ma'am, fuck your orders. Let your brain trust of engineers there know we have arrested the spin from Morrigan, and we're damn well going to move her onto the intercept course. I'm Brigade, ma'am, we don't settle for second best. Hooah."

I was so fired when we get... if we get home. It would be latrine duty for, well, forever, I'm sure. Dang it, I wish Mother were here, she'd know what to do now, I was sure of it. She was great at unorthodox thinking, or inspiring me to think outside the box.

Hmm... I checked some numbers and cocked an eyebrow. That was encouraging, I headed to the engineering bay and started checking gear and docking systems. I hesitated as I moved past the vault, incoherent whispers in my head teased at salvation, if only I were to let the power of the forge free. It promised me the world, and all I had to do was to accept what it could give me. It would have its freedom and I could solve all the problems of...

I shook my head and exhaled, wiping a cold sweat from my brow. It was so seductive, like Fae glamour, but it was just as manipulative as the Fae too. I got the impression that it just wanted to be free and would promise the world to achieve that.... but it had no morality. It wanted to be free to create and to destroy, and to be... whole again? Had the Forge of Creation been alive?

It tried to ensnare me again and I stumbled backwards and turned to walk quickly away, just to run into Oberon. It was like hitting a ceramic alloy wall. He looked down at me, his piercing Fae eyes going through me like they were reading my soul.

Then he turned away, “Our rest period has expired. It's time to finish the mission.”

I nodded and hustled after him. He paused at the ladder and said without looking at me, curiosity painting his tone, “You denied the call. Impressive.” Then he started to climb.

As I followed I shared, “Only because it creeps me the fuck out.”

He chuckled and then asked as we climbed, “Did you find a solution? We'll have to tell her soon.”

Exhaling, I shared as I nodded, “I know. I'm working on something, just need to crunch some numbers.”

He just nodded then said, “Well that is for another time. Right now, we have to ensure the survival of the people on the Worldship.”

Fifteen minutes later, the magi-tech engine linkages were quadrupling the thrust of the small World-Drive on the tug as we kept increasing the vectoring power. The ship was shaking and creaking, the ancient mega-structure groaning like old bones as the New Hope shoved against more mass than it was ever designed to move so quickly. If we had more time, she could eventually move Morrigan where we needed, but we didn't have the fuel or time for that. So here we were. I was praying to some old Norse gods I had read about back in University that the magi-tech linkages would hold.

Against my wishes, Mac and Rory started feeding their power into the core with the Focus again. They kept draining themselves over and over, it couldn't be good for them or their magic.

Twenty minutes later, the throttle was maxed, engine output was so far above redline I was surprised we hadn't gone critical and vaporized ourselves and Morrigan in the process. I had to lower my visor and engage the sound dampening talisman of my scatter armor. But even so, the massive engine whining, the protesting of the tug's superstructure, and the vibrations translating through the vessel causing a shaking thrum, was almost deafening. I didn't know how the two Fae were handling it with their sensitive hearing... then again, they were probably using magic to save their ears.

Just when I thought New Hope would shake herself apart, I stepped to the window to look at the rock face just inches from me and I growled out a challenge, “Come on! Move you bitch!”

And then... she moved.

The numbers in my helmet started changing as we altered the trajectory of the massive world that was determined to kill us all. The changes were miniscule, but they were changes. Oberon bled into his Mac form and he and Rory relaxed as they stopped feeding their power into the engines.

Then as the minutes, then hours ticked past, with Morrigan's will broken, she was heeding our demands. It would take a day or two, but we would get her to where she needed to be and accelerated to the speed needed for capture.

We had done it!

When we finally slowed, to eject the asteroid along her way, the noise level dropped enough we could communicate with each other without typed messages on our virtual consoles. And dozens of messages started streaming in from home. While the World-Drive was active, the interference was too great for even magic backed communication transmissions to get through to us.

I looked at my crew-mates, “So, should we see just how much trouble we're in, disobeying direct orders?”

Mac grinned and said, “I'm a Remnant, not subject to the laws of the World.”

“Coward.”

“Guilty.”

Rory muttered, “Children.” Then she said, “We should eat, and hydrate, none of us even left the bridge during that. Then we can see what President Yang has to say, shall we?”

I nodded slowly, nervously, then shared, “Sounds good, besides, there's something Mac and I need to share.”

He looked stricken, “Throw me under the bus with you Knith?”

I wondered what a bus was, and then another pang of loss shot through me as I thought, “Mother would know.”

Shoving the man's shoulder I said, “Of course.”

Then I just about melted when my girl rested her fingers primly in the crook of my arm. I may have sighed a little as I placed a hand on top of hers then led her to the mess.

CHAPTER 19

Home

Just as we finished eating, Aurora was standing, hissing out at us, eyes crackling with icy blue fire that was colder than the vacuum of space, “You're just telling me this now? How bad is it?”

Mac looked at me since I had been working on it. “We lost most of our environmental systems, and the main oxygen tank ruptured into space when Morrigan threw her tantrum. There was air enough from environmental systems left for one of us to survive the trip back home. But I've coaxed marginal air scrubbing from the systems, salvaged the tanks from our EVA suits and the compressors in the airlock pressurization tanks for two people if we keep the oxygenation low. I'm looking for other ways to generate oxygen and scrub the atmosphere.”

Mac looked to be doing some calculations in his head, it was the same look that Rory got when she was solving problems in her lab. He was shaking his head, “With the three of us consuming air while we look for solutions, we have only a day or two before we cross the threshold for two to survive the trip home.”

I could see where my girl got her intelligence. The man's mind was like a computer... not as proficient as Mother's but still, to do all the calculations on the fly like that. But I've come to expect it from both the old space jockey and Aurora.

She exhaled in frustration. “Show us what you've done so far, maybe we can help eak a little more performance from the systems, and maybe the artifact can provide them more power if it is needed. We won't need it anymore as we've successfully accomplished the goal of this mission.”

I swallowed, she was really mad at me for not disclosing this to her sooner. But I didn't want her distracted while we moved the stubborn space rock into position to save our fleet. And I wanted to see if I could solve the problem before it even became an issue.

After stepping them through the systems I bastardized, and the other systems I either cannibalized or modified to perform life support tasks, they both seemed a little surprised and impressed. Mac was saying, “You've a knack for problem solving, Knith. Some of this work is inspired. Using the holding tanks for the airlock pressurizing systems, it's not pure oxygen but it will virtually double the breathable air. Jury-rigging work like this is worthy of the Remnant fixers. And utilizing all but the water needed to survive the trip back to extract oxygen from... very nice.”

A thought was forming in my mind as they crunched numbers as they tweaked my systems. Then Rory sighed. “Unless we can find another source of oxygen, then we are faced with a hard choice.”

I asked, “What about extracting water from Morrigan then extracting the oxygen from it?”

They were both shaking their heads, “The air you use on the spacewalks to gather materials would be more than could be extracted. We'd need almost twenty three tons of rock to extract the water needed."

So there was one choice, I hated it because it was actually one ot the things that scared me most. Queen Mab had threatened to do it on many occasions and it gave me nightmares for days. I sighed heavily and said, "There's nothing for it then. If you can just do as your mother does and freeze me into an ice sculpture until we get back to the Leviathan, then thaw me. Then we all survive. It's the only solution."

My voice had started shaking at the prospect. Rory had told me what it was like to be living ice, conscious and aware while Mab's punishment was met out. The cold is unbearable but you cannot even shiver because your body is a solid mass of frozen magic so you just stand there seeing only what is in front of you because you can't move your eyes. You don't sleep, you don't breathe, you don't get tired or hungry, you just are and it slowly eats away at your sanity because you are just an object.

And whatever physical or mental state you were in at the time the curse was cast, is the state you remain in. So if you had a headache or a painful injury, you just bear that pain until you are released. Or in the case of one of Mab's lovers she caught cheating on her, she had frozen them during climax so that pleasure has become an eternal torture for them for thousands of years in her bed chambers where she caught them.

This would only be a few weeks, as our trip back would be less than half the time of our journey here. But still, it scared the hells out of me, especially since there are rumors that sometimes the process cannot be reversed if the victim loses their mind while frozen in place. I have learned that most Fae rumors are true, since the Greater Fae cannot lie. It was very rare for them to hear a story second hand that was untrue, so almost all their gossip had at least a good helping of truth as its basis.

Scarier than being stuck forever that way, was the fact that Mab was, how would Graz put it? Batshit crazy? And she has taken an interest in me, so if she saw me that way she might not allow Rory to reverse the process and she'd have me decorating her chambers.

Aurora was by my side, one hand on my hip, the other caressing my cheek as her eyes glittered with... wonder? “Oh Knith. Your bravery knows no bounds. Always first to volunteer, first to sacrifice for others. Even those not of your race. It is one of the singular things which make you unique, that makes me love you. There is nobody like Knith Shade, Brigade Enforcer of the Beta-Stack.”

She kissed me gently and shook her head as Mac rumbled out, “It would work, we...”

My girl laid her head on my shoulder and said, “No, it would not work. As brave and noble as the idea is, Knith has partial magic immunity.”

Mac huffed out a breath and said, “I thought it was something like that, but you and your mothers keep your secrets tightly kept. Not even the palace guards who are privy to Knith's secret will speak of it. And how she broke Sindri's thrall... I have operated under the assumption of it but now that you've verified it... It must never become public knowledge. Hunter parties from the various preternatural races would be sent out, they would see her as a danger.”

I sputtered, “What do you mean a danger? I'm no threat to anyone... unless you break the law on the world.” Hmm, there was that odd mention again, of the Queens both being her mother even though only Mab was. I still found that portion of their society quite alien.

Rory shared, “When the magic races were still young, and mankind began to spread across the Earth, their only defense against the huge numbers of Humans that claimed the lands of Fairie as their own, was magic. Old hidebound elders from most of the races, even fringe castes of the Greater Fae, would see it as a danger beyond words if their only weapon was negated. Papa is right, just the rumor of your immunity would have hunter killer parties looking to eliminate you as a threat.”

“But that's murder. Premeditated at that.”

She nodded, “Yes, it is. But they would see the threat to their people as greater than the punishments the law would levy against them if they could eliminate the threat.”

Wait a minute. I heard rumors of hunter parties connected with the disturbances on the Leviathan. And Aurora would be exhausted every time she came home whenever she vanished. Was she... was she intercepting these hunters before they could get to me? Mother fairy humper, we really, really, needed to talk when we got back home. This is serious stuff, and if the Brigade caught wind of it, everyone involved, even my girl could be arrested for their involvement.

My mind, rewound a minute and my eyes narrowed as I prompted, “Wait, you said it wouldn't work on me. Even if it wore off every few days, you could just re-cast, right?”

Mac looked interested in the answer too as he eyed me up and down like it was the first time he was seeing me. She shared as she shook her head slowly, “You build up an immunity every time a spell is re-cast upon you, Knith. Like a thrall glamour, you barely broke mother's. But broke Sindri's much more easily. It is like you gain a resistance.”

She shrugged and offered, “You do not even notice the don't look here I have on my guards at all times now, and see them plain as day. None of my don't look here's work on you anymore because you've been exposed so many times you've built up a resistance. And the same would be true for anyone else, once exposed multiple times, theirs would be useless too.”

Her tone was dejected as she held her hands, palm up and provided, “So each time we crystallized your cells with raw winter magic, you would recover faster and faster until it didn't work.”

I shook my head, “No, that can't be right. Your mother and Titania have been marking me, well, hundreds of times now, and it finally faded. I haven't built a resistance to that.”

She smirked and Mac chuckled and offered, “Because it is still only the first time. They must just be reinforcing the original curses in some manner. The next time they mark you that way will require more power from them as it will be harder for it to stick to you.”

“Oh.”

Then I sobered. “That was my last idea. There isn't anything else we can do then. Maybe Doc will have an idea. We can message him in the next data burst and...”

Rory smiled almost sadly at me as she said over her shoulder to her father, “Knith Shade of Beta-Stack does not know how to surrender. She fights even when the outcome is bleak.” Then she whispered, “Oh how I love you my brave Don Quixote. But there is a simple solution you have not considered.”

I furrowed my brow, I've gone over hundreds of possibilities, what was she... She kissed me and winked as she let go of me and took three steps back, right into the airlock. I started to step toward her as she hit the emergency override with a blast of icy magic disabling the controls on this side. I was yelling at her, “Rory! What are you doing!?”

She smiled nervously as she grabbed the equipment netting and said, "See you two on the other side." Then she hit the outer door control. I just looked on in horror as she clung there as the vacuum equalized in the space. Her eyes widened as she started gasping for air that wasn't there.

By the gods! She was... she was putting herself through the horror of spacing like Mac had described to me. She'd be aware the full time like one of Mab's sculptures as she froze solid over time. But... she was saving me. I felt useless, it was supposed to be me! She didn't need to endure a living hell for me. It was my job to protect her.

I pounded on the window of the door, knowing how futile it was since she wouldn't hear me. Someone caught my hand in a grip of steel. I looked back to see Mac had shed his Human guise and I stared into the face of Oberon himself. He told me, "Let her have this. Don't diminish her sacrifice. She will survive this, but I cannot let her go through it alone. It is terrifying, even to my kind."

He smiled sadly, and it was devastating on such a beautiful face. He said to me, "Bring us home Knith Shade. I must comfort my daughter."

"Wh-what?"

He smiled sadly one last time and I was almost knocked on my ass by the wave of power that flowed off of him, my magnetic boots were the only thing that kept me on my feet. Then the being of crackling electric power and magic just... well, he just stepped through the wall like it wasn't even there.

He moved to Aurora who was clawing at her throat in a panic. He wrapped his arms around her, and she grabbed onto him and calmed down and grasped at him desperately. After a minute, she was calm and no longer gasping. And the two turned to me, my girl in her father's arms, and the outer door closed on some unseen command, leaving them secured in the airlock as I stood... alone... as I watched them just drift there.

I didn't leave the airlock, and Rory stopped moving, losing her mobility around forty five minutes later. And King Oberon just held her, his eyes on me the whole time, then after twenty two hours, he too stopped moving, I knew that my girl, who was going through what amounted to torture, was frozen solid by then, and Oberon would join her by tomorrow.

I could feel the gravity they had created in the New Hope fade with them. I sighed, placed a hand on the window and started moving. I was glad that there was no gravity now, because my legs ached. I was so hungry and needed to sleep. Both of which I felt guilty for as the two Greater Fae stood unmoving in the airlock.

But first... I headed to the bridge and looked at the controls. A patchwork of ancient tech and new magi-tech panels. “Ok, Knith. Just like in the simulators... without the crashing. How hard could it be?”

A minute later I was cussing in seven different languages, thinking I'd likely need a change of undergarments as I wrestled the mammoth beast onto our return trajectory. By the time the little red course indicator merged with the little green indicator, I was even more exhausted than before as the adrenaline of basically surfing on the wake of a world-drive's thrust worked its way out of my system.

Ok, now I just had to set the... I noted the big, huge, virtual control button which read “Autopilot”. Son of a... where the hells had my head been? I tapped it and saw the course was already laid in as well as the engine cutoff sequence in seventy three hours, and the thrust vectoring for the various burns required for rendezvous with home. I rolled my eyes and activated it. I felt a minor course correction and I grumped at the ship, “Whatever.”

Then I dragged myself to the mess then the racks, where I picked Graz's cocoon in one hand and cradled it to my chest in my arms as I laid down for the most fitful sleep of my life.

EPILOGUE

I was actually going to miss the man. I smiled and grasped forearms with Doc, the man was still learning all he could about the culture, and society, as well as the magi-tech improvements on the Worldship since Exodus five millennia ago.

He felt this journey, that sounded one part spiritual and one part curiosity about this amazing world we all lived inside that he had helped build. This was the future to him, a future he had never been fated to see. It was a rebellious AI that ran the Leviathan who had talked him into coming with us, with her so she wouldn't be alone.

So this grand adventure he was setting off on by foot, he called a walkabout. He was going to visit every ring, and every community, every city, every town on every ring, and every stack of the Leviathan. To see how life is thriving, to learn about it, experience it, and the people who have forged the life's work of the people who dreamed up an artificial world to ferry life from Earth to a new home, into a reality.

I straightened his collar for him and smiled at the positively antique style of clothing he chose to wear. I kissed him on the cheek and said, “Things won't be the same here without you.”

He gave a cocky grin. “Ain't that the truth?” He winked then said as he squinted one eye, “Umm... I've got to pee. Hold this for me? Be back in a flash.”

All of us gathered to see him off chuckled as he handed his rucksack off to Beta, the redheaded human-looking avatar with the librarian's glasses and a figure that looked suspiciously like my Aurora's. I won't lie to you, but damn, Mother had crafted a special kind of sexy for her Beta-Stack avatar this time.

I can't believe it had already been six months since our not so triumphant return to the world. The maneuvering thruster systems had shorted out on our approach, and the fleet went tearing past us, New Hope barely missing the ring stacks as I was pulling on the yoke as hard as I could and firing the world-drive for two seconds to avoid impact.

That sent us spiraling off, and two full squadrons from Ready Squadron had to give chase to their extreme range and were able to harpoon us with hundreds of elandium alloy tow cables to tow us back to the Leviathan. To my eternal embarrassment, the first live voice I had heard that wasn't just a recording in the daily data bursts from home, was my ex, Myra, who had purred out on coms, “Well well well, look at what we've caught people, a wayward Brigade Enforcer. Don't worry Brigade, Ready Squad is here. Going our way.”

“Brigade eats Ready Squadron for breakfast, lady,” I growled out in mortification.

She chuckled then said with a touch of incredulity in her tone, “Mab's tits, Knith. The ship looks torn to shit. You were able to move that asteroid and fly back home in it?”

I shook my head and said plainly, "No, as you can see, we needed rescuing..." I trailed off and cut coms to fight off an anxiety attack. We? No... me. I had been alone for weeks and it was all I could do to keep it together and not start sobbing at being home. I keyed my mic again and said, trying to stop it from sounding like pleading, "Get this piece of floating junk docked for me, I have to make sure Aurora is ok."

Every day I would get up, tuck the cocoon under my pillow, then exercise using my armor in resistance mode so I had something to work against so I didn't lose muscle and bone density in zero-g. Then I would go for a run through the ship using my mag boots and the micro thrusters in the suit to keep me on the decks.

Then after eating, I would go down to the airlock and sit there, just watching Rory and Oberon. I read to her from the library of books Mother had thoughtfully included in my suit's data core along with the music. I don't know if she could hear me or not, but I had to do something. She was suffering... for me... reading for her was the only fucking thing I could do and it was eating away at me.

Late each day when I headed back up to eat and sleep and do it all over again, the artifact would call out to me. Enticing me, promising me everything and nothing. And I realized something... it was lonely. It wanted someone to use its power so that it could feel some connection to anything, to anyone, no matter how temporarily.

And after that epiphany, I took some time to sit outside the vault and tried to let it know that while I wouldn't use it... I would be there each day to share in its isolation. That's when I learned the most frightening thing in all my years. This insane idea I had that magic was sentient, or at least the fragments of the Forge were at the very least, an advanced AI proved not to be all in my head.

Because after I had made that silent pact... I felt acceptance, and the artifact stopped trying to subvert me, and use me to use it. Instead, I felt... I felt the void, its void, and the eternity of eternities of emptiness, a vague impression of the other pieces of itself scattered across so many worlds, giving life to each in an attempt to have that life reunite the pieces, to make it whole again.

Again, I felt insignificant, because just as I could do nothing for the woman I loved, I could do nothing for this... entity who was... alone.

We docked, ironically with the help of a dozen small skin jockey tugs, and the umbilicals were connected, flooding the ship with fresh air and sucking away the stale, oily, stagnant air I had been breathing for so long. The moment we had green lights, I blew the airlock door and rushed to my girl.

Queen Mab and Titania appeared beside me in a whump of magic as I laid a hand on Rory's frozen form. The Summer and Winter Ladies both glared at me as they touched Rory and Oberon, and they were gone. And I just sat on the deck and waited as damage control personnel, med-techs, and decontamination crews swarmed in, and I let a single sob shake my shoulders before I was pushing away the med-techs as they insisted, “Come with us Lieutenant Shade, you need to be...”

“No! Out of my way.”

I made my way back up to my bunk, pushing technicians out of the way in the corridors until I got to Graz. I cradled her and then allowed myself to be pulled along by the med-techs who had followed me as I tucked my friend into a belt pouch. When they were insisting I get on a mag-sled stretcher in the equipment bay, I hesitated at the Greater Fae who were trying to open the vault, but they were being rebuffed by something powerful.

I overheard the Fae sounding afraid as they spoke to someone on coms, “We need more senior Fae in here, the artifact won't let us in. What? No, Titania's panties man, don't ask the Queen to come, are you insane?” They were afraid that the piece from the Ka'Infinitum wasn't listening to them. They knew. The Greater Fae knew that the fragments held some sort of life.

I told the medics, “Just a moment.” Then I stepped over to the door which was locked by the most complex swirling circles of magic with imbued spell-work and sigils in both Fae and Elvish, but there was another set of sigils that looked to be like the ones etched on the artifact that seemed to loop though the Fae's workings, locking them down to prevent them from doing what they were designed to do.

One Fae Lord warned me, “Human, step away or you will be removed. This is...”

I whirled and was in his face, hissing, "You see this badge? It says I am the law here, Brigade..." Then I gave a clear indication of who had authority here. "...citizen."

"You lost control of it, now shut the hells up. A little honey works better than vinegar. You'd think a race who was eternal, a race created by these very artifacts would know this."

I reached a hand forward toward the spellwork on the door, and the man actually grabbed my arm, I winced, even with my armor protecting me, I was reminded just how strong the Fae are. I sighed and before he could react, I grabbed a mag-band from my belt and slapped it on his other arm and said as I glared into his silvery violet eyes, "Lockdown."

Caught by surprise, he let go of me as his other arm was yanked to the deck with ten G's of force. He'd be able to overcome that in a few seconds but that's all I needed. "Consider yourself bound by law for assaulting an enforcer of the Brigade. Now do you want the artifact or not?"

The Fae lady watched the entire thing and she looked from the man who was struggling to stand and me. Some sort of recognition flashed through her eyes and she just inclined her head. I knew the Artifacts supposedly could only be handled by the most powerful of the Greater Fae. That is why these two were here, to retrieve it immediately and return into the Ka'Infinitum. And I've seen a man literally undone just by gazing upon them. But I was going by my gut. And my gut told me... that I'd be ok.

I placed my palm on the door, and all the swirling magic rushed to and spun around my hand. “The shard and I have come to an understanding.” And the door opened and blinding, but beautiful and terrible light flooded the doorway.

I stepped inside and the shard gave the impression of moving back a step, though it never physically moved from the cradle it sat in. “It's ok now,” I said as I reached out after seeing the Fae Lady couldn't step into the room, blocked as she was by a coherent wall of magic.

I could see the infinite worlds and time unending and all the wonder and terror of creation in the light. It was the most beautiful sight to see again, and I felt... the only word I could think of as I basked in the terrifying serenity, was blessed. I had cried the first time I was introduced to the Ka'Infinitum, and I did so now. While not as overwhelming as seeing the artifacts all together, it was still almost about to start unraveling my physical and spiritual reality, being too much to comprehend, and leaving me as a dusting of random energy for it to absorb. But it held back.

With a sad smile, I said, “I'm going to return you to the other shards on the world now. I know you want all the other shards too, but I don't know where they are. At least you won't be alone anymore.”

I closed my eyes, and said a prayer to any of the gods who may be watching, hells, I may have been praying to the Forge itself, that I wasn't just mad, and was imagining all of the impressions I had been getting, then I placed a hand on the artifact. It was warm to the touch and I felt the tears flowing on my cheek again. Resignation with a touch of gratefulness was what I felt flowing into me.

Nodding, I stepped out of the room. The Fae Lady had a cube that looked to be made of magic ready. Her eyes glittered in a desire that she pushed away as a tear rolled down her cheek as the light spilled upon her. She had a strong will. I placed the artifact in the box and she closed it with a quick chant.

It was as if a huge pressure was lifted from the air and I could breathe freely again. “Get it to the other artifacts safely?” I asked her. She just nodded and left, I never got her name, but I saw the understanding in her eyes.

I placed a hand on the shoulder of the Fae Lord who was struggling in a shuffling walk after her, his arm trying to drag him to the deck, his other hand trying to break the band on his arm. “Whoa there Zippy the garden squirrel. Where do you think you're going? You're bound by law.”

He glared at me and said in the officious tone I was used to hearing from the Greater Fae, “Who do you think you are? I'm with the Fae council and...”

“And you laid hands on an Enforcer. You have Fairy shit for brains or something? Mab sent out the decree to remind both courts that they were subject to the same laws as everyone else. And who do I think I am?” I growled out, “I'm Nobody.”

The Satyr medics were looking at me expectantly. Just hold up goat faces, I'll be with you in a moment.

The Fae Lord was getting control of his frustration and anger, realizing I wasn't afraid of him nor any retaliation he may try to get by punishing my home stack. But then he got distracted as he looked from me to the now-empty vault room. “You're a mortal... a Human. You were able to touch an artifact, to hold it. How is that possible? No mortal being can even behold them for long without being undone.”

I told him the truth. “Because it and I had an understanding. And it knew that no matter what it promised, I was never going to use its power nor be consumed by it.” Then I told him flat out, “I don't know if I fully understand or agree with what you Fae are doing with the artifacts, but I do know loneliness, and something has to be done about that. You use them as tools, the same way you used Mother. But you don't take into account that even if they are life we don't understand or can fathom, artificial or not, that emotion or concepts like them should be taken into account in the way you use them.”

Then I cocked my head at a thought that started forming in my head. “Even though the artifacts are just fragments of the Forge of Creation, they were what gave life to your race. Has anyone ever considered that maybe the way you use them has more to do with your people's inability to procreate anymore, than the assumption it is just because we are not on Earth anymore?”

He blinked, shock on his face, then his brow creased as he genuinely looked as if he was considering my words, nodding absently as he processed it. “I'm going to release you now with a warning, but if you do anything asinine again like this in the future, I'll be the one arresting you. Do we have an understanding Lord...”

The man straightened as I reached for his wrist. “Lord Percival.” Oh... Summer Court, I hadn't expected that, Titania's third-born. Shit, she was going to hate me even more now.

I grabbed the mag-band and paused and said, “Lord Percival. Now say, thank you Enforcer Shade.”

He smirked like I had told a great joke, then he realized I hadn't released the mag-band. “Oh, you're serious.”

With a shrug, I said, “Your choices are to thank me or be arrested. Choose.” I know I was evil, but I had a super shitty few months and I just wasn't in any sort of mood to listen to the holier than thou Fae Fairy shit. And thanking a Greater Fae was tantamount to admitting that you were in their debt, and they used that ruthlessly and a simple thank you could have you in their debt for life.

He narrowed his eyes and did what Fae did. He bargained with me, “A favor.”

I nodded. “Your word?”

“Done.”

“Done, but I'm not sealing the contract with a kiss. I'll just use your honor as Third of the Summer Court.”

His scowl was replaced with a sly smile as I released him, and he looked from the vault to me to ask, “Are you sure you're not Fae, Enforcer?”

I told him as I stepped over and laid down on the stretcher, “One hundred percent, grade-A Human.”

“Shall we meet again.”

“Oh gods, I hope not.” Then I grinned.

My eyes widened, and in a panic looked to the cocoon I had tucked into a belt pouch. It was still warm. I hadn't even thought about Graz being with me when I went into the vault. I sighed in relief.

So Morrigan had killed Beta, tried to kill Graz, almost killed the rest of us, and almost destroyed the Tug. But I was home now, and now a Fae Lord owed me a favor, maybe today wouldn't be such a bad day.

As I was moved into a medical transport in the Trunk, I realized that something had been missing since we docked. I said into my helmet, “Mother?” Why hadn't she been talking to me or even greeted me once we docked?

A relief I cannot begin to explain flooded through me when the speakers in the corridor then in the transport burst to life, and a frantic Mother was blurting, “Knith! Oh, thank the gods! I haven't been able to reach you through your armor's coms. Something is overwriting many of your armor's systems. Are you all alright?

What am I saying, of course, you're not ok. It must have been a nightmare. I'll be with you the whole way to med-tech. I..."

I sighed and interrupted her rapid-fire babbling. "By the gods have I missed you too, lady." Then I added, "Love you."

She sighed and said, "Love you too Knith. I don't know why, since you're always rushing into dangerous situations. My heart can't take it."

I grinned and said, "Well then, you're in luck. I got you a new heart, it'll just take a year or four to catch it though." I paused when I looked at the medics who just looked shocked and stunned at the conversation I was having with the world we all lived in. I think they thought I wasn't right in the head.

Smirking to them and pointing at the roof, I said, "Redheads? What ya gonna do?"

The next few days had been nerve-wracking, once I was cleared by medical, Mother had my Tac-Bike waiting for me outside of the facility and I must have broken every speeding law to get to the A-Ring and to the Winter Palace, Ha'Real, to see my girl. Mab had refused all calls from me and nobody was telling me if she was ok or not.

The palace guard tried to stop me from entering, but I glared at Delphine of House Kryn, captain of the Queen's Guard, my sometimes friend, sometimes adversary. My... frenemy. And I growled out, "Do you seriously think you can keep me from the woman I love, Delphine?" I was a little shocked by how cold and menacing my voice sounded. And her eyes were moving from mine to my hands where they hovered near my sides, by the collapsible cold iron batons as my fingers twitched.

She sighed and inclined her head to me in capitulation. “Mab will have my hide. She gave specific orders to...”

“Tell her I hit you.”

She said, “You know the Fae cannot lie. I...” Her head snapped back as my fist lashed out to strike her nose.

Owwww! It was like hitting a wall.

The other guards lunged their pikes toward me but she waved them off with a chuckle as she straightened the broken nose, wiping away the blood and I heard the crinkle of the cartilage healing itself.

She turned her head, though her eyes were still tracking me as I stepped past her. “You all saw it, she hit me and got past me. How are we to stop one so determined?”

She was good people at times. And she called after me as I reached the doors of Ha'Real my intent burning in my mind, a destination in mind for the palace to read from me. It had taken me months to figure out how sometimes it would take me ten minutes traveling the halls to get to my desk outside Aurora's office, and sometimes I'd step through the courtyard doors and directly into it. As with everything with Fae magic, it is all about intent.

I didn't want to deal with any other overzealous guards, so I was picturing Rory's bed chamber and stepped directly into them. Just to hit a wall. Ok, not a wall, but Mab had somehow known I was stepping through because I had stepped right into her outstretched hand. I oofed, and the Winter Lady turned her eyes from the sleeping form on the bed and turned her terrifyingly cruel eyes upon me.

She said as I watched the Summer Lady over her shoulder, sitting on the bed, wiping Aurora's angelic face with a cloth, “The guards were given instructions that the Winter Maiden not be disturbed.”

I shrugged and said distractedly, “I hit them.” Then I whispered, “Is she..?”

Queen Mab softened and dropped her hand as she looked back at her daughter. “She's fine. She's strong. It takes a week or two to fully recover from hibernation sickness. And none can see her in a weakened state, especially Summer. They will take advantage of and try to best her.”

Blinking at that, I looked at the Summer Queen who just grinned at that statement. I stared in confusion since Titania basically was Summer. She shared from where she was tending my girl, who looked so tranquil and peaceful asleep there on the sinfully soft bed, like some porcelain doll who was arranged just so to project an innocence none of the Fae truly possessed, “If one of my court were to best her, then all the better. But it is my duty to the children of the Ladies of the divided courts, to protect them and care for them until they can protect themselves.”

I blinked in surprise as Mab joined her and cupped her rival's cheek lovingly. I'll never get used to how these women, who hated each other to the core of their beings, also loved each other with the same fire. They had been lovers once upon a time when mankind was young, and I don't really understand how their culture works enough to make sense of the dichotomy. You never knew from one second to the next if they were about to stab each other in the back, or drop into bed and work out their passion in ways that would make even Aphrodite blush.

My understanding here was that the thirteen firstborns of each of the Queens were regarded in some way to be the children of both. I believe it is a power thing, one thing the Greater Fae understands the most. The twenty-six firstborn have the potential to be the next rulers of the Divided courts if they amass enough power to unseat their mother. And that made them precious to them, even if it were a double-edged blade since it also made the children the most dangerous threat to the Queens as well.

Whatever odd relationship they all had, I could see that both the Queens loved Rory. Neither of them stopped me, even though they glared when I sat on the other side of the bed and reached a hand out to stroke Rory's silken hair.

Her eyes fluttered open, and they turned to me as recognition pushed away the last of the sleep, and she smiled widely as she sat quickly to pull me into a tight hug. “Knith! You're here! Mother wouldn't allow me to contact you until I was recovered.”

I gasped and patted her arm as I heard my bones creaking. “You're... crushing... me... love.”

She giggled as she relaxed her desperate hug a bit. “Oh. Sorry, my Knith.”

Rory released me and then stole a heated kiss that had my toes curling and my special places heating. Then I was gasping as I was physically lifted from her by the collar of my helmet by one hand by Mab. She set me aside on my feet and pointed at the door. “You have seen her, and see she is fine, now leave us. You will be summoned when she reaches her full power again.”

I huffed in exasperation but inclined my head. “Fine. I love you Aurora.”

My girl beamed at me like she had won a prize. And I sighed and turned to the door, just to find Titania directly in front of me, kissing me. Her power flooded my very being, imprinting itself on my soul as she seemed to struggle a moment before it took hold. She released me as I gasped, knowing without checking that my upper lip was aflame again. She said, “You didn't think you'd get out of here without wearing my mark did you Knith Shade of Beta-Stack?”

Mother fairy humper, I had hoped that they had forgotten about... another set of lips were on mine, and I heard the sizzle of ice on fire as Mab did the same, her magic freezing me to my core. I stumbled in a bit of a haze as she ushered me to the door. I licked my lips, feeling the fire and slick ice on them as I stumbled out into the corridor.

The guards at the door seemed shocked and surprised when I caught my balance as they spun to look at the closing doors. I looked up to see a grinning Oberon leaning against the wall, arms crossed over his chest. He gave an ironic wave with a single motion of his arm. I smirked and leaned against the wall beside him.

“They allowed you to see her?”

I chuckled. “They didn't have a choice, I know how the doors work in this place, and the lockouts don't work on me.”

He chuckled at that then asked, “How is she?”

I looked over at him. “She's fine. Recovering. But you don't look any worse for wear. You're already recovered?”

He looked pleased that his daughter was ok, then shook his head. “Hibernation sickness has just about run its course, I'm not at one hundred percent yet.” When the guards straightened almost imperceptibly at the implied weakness, he spoke to them, not me, “But even if I were at death's door, I still have more than enough power to deal with the likes of you two.” His eyes glowed with crackling power to punctuate it.

Shaking my head I asked him, “Doesn't it ever get old? This fucked up game of power you Fae live by? Looking for weaknesses to take advantage of to advance? For what reason?”

The man chuckled at me, and pointed out, "Of course it does. Why do you think I left the Divided Courts, to hide among the people of the world?"

"Ok. Fair point." Then I pointed out, "Aurora doesn't look for advantage or leverage against weakness."

"That, young Knith, is why she is the jewel of my heart. She lives in the world of the Greater Fae, but she strives to be... better."

Huh. Maybe there was hope for the old man after all.

From there, I made my way back home to rest. Home. I hadn't realized how much I had missed it. And Graz' family must have been going insane with worry. I had word sent to them when I was confined to medical, but I wouldn't entrust the cocoon to anyone to bring it to them. I wouldn't let anyone touch it, and wouldn't let the medics scan it. They were intensely intrigued by it since a Sprite had never done this in all the time the Leviathan had been in flight.

The moment I stepped through the door, I was mauled by a family of flying buzz bombers as the family... I thought of them as my family now... zipped around, leaving trails of dust behind them as they all chittered and bombarded me with dozens of questions. And the kids were trying to drop a chain of daisies around my neck.

I helped with the flower necklace they had crafted for my return and just held one hand out and the kids landed on my palm. I looked to Graz' spouses, and said to Mitzy, since I knew she was in charge of the mated tri's family after Graz, "She's right here."

Reaching carefully into my belt packs I withdrew the cocoon and held it out to them. They buzzed over and grabbed it and buzzed into my sleeping quarters and into the nightstand as the children squeaked out questions. “What is space like?”

“Was Morrigan like our new home?”

“Is space bigger than a Big?”

We were rejoined by their parents, as I set them all on the table, as I started stripping out of my armor to relax. I was home and it felt as if my nightmare of a journey had finally ended. Mitzy shared, “The Fae council want to know the moment Graz emerges. There have only been two Greater Sprites in all of history. We Sprites don't normally live long enough, we have violent lives. We lost the only Greater Sprite on the world in the great sickness.”

“Greater Sprite?”

She nodded in excitement. “Only the oldest and wisest of us when we've gathered enough energy, go into stasis as our bodies change. Our Grazzie will be a Greater Sprite! It's so very exciting.” She spun in place, dust from her moth-like wings spraying out cutely. I could see why Graz married the adorable woman.

Huh. Now my curiosity was killing me. “How long before she emerges?”

Her husband shrugged and shared, “Nobody really knows. Predators usually devour them before they can emerge. Only two have ever survived so it could be hours, weeks, years, or centuries.”

Mitzy said, “But there is so much power in the stasis pod. We know that it's not normal, it tastes like the Princess and the King of Faerie. So I'd bet on sooner than later.”

I nodded and headed to the bedroom for a change of clothes as I started to shed my skinsuit. Mitzy squeaked in alarm, “You must be tired and hungry.” She whistled shrilly and called out when the children burst into the air in a cloud of wing dust as she called out, “Children, get food for Knith! Enough for a Big!”

Then she zoomed off with them toward the kitchen. I had to smile. I felt loved and doted upon at times by the family who had sort of forced their way into my life... literally. I couldn't imagine a time without them.

Fast forward to now, six months was the answer as to how long Graz would remain in her cocoon. And Doc had postponed his walkabout until he was sure the little flying annoyance was ok. I seriously liked the man.

I fidgeted with the medals on my dress armor. And Graz chimed out, “Stop fiddling with them, Knith! You stupid Bigs sure fixate on things.”

I smirked, loving the annoyingly sarcastic voice in my ear again. And she looked spectacular! The Greater Fae saw lesser Fae like Sprites and Fairies as pests, vermin, though they enjoyed the Fairies in their gardens purely for the aesthetics. They were dumb as rocks, but the Fairies had an unnatural beauty to them, with gossamer wings that sparkled in translucent colors. But they tossed out any

Sprites who dared to sully their gardens with their dull, ugly moth wings.

But Graz. Just wow. I mean, if this was what a Greater Sprite looked like, the Fae should be rethinking their shallow views, since my annoying buzzing companion put the beauty of the Fairies to shame. The Fae should be helping and encouraging more Sprites to the chrysalis stage.

Graz glowed with a golden light, and veins of magic gold spun across her skin in ever-changing patterns, making her look almost ethereal. But her wings... her wings were twice the size they were before, with impossible colors and that otherworldly golden glow cycling on them. Like some sort of butterfly to the gods. And I could actually feel the power emanating off of her. Sprites normally have too little for me to feel, but hers now was five or ten times what a Sprite held, and it tasted of honey and ice.

All the Fae Lords and Ladies were clamoring to get time with her to try to convince her that joining their houses would be mutually beneficial, but she would always respond, "Buzz off! I'm of house Shade. Someone has to take care of the dumb Big or she might stick her finger in a power port or something."

It was so good to have her back and insulting me again.

I still couldn't believe I was a captain of the Brigade now. I got a severe dress-down in the endless debriefings for the mission, by the President herself. She had knocked me back to Private for disobeying direct orders. Assured me that a strong letter of reprimand was being affixed to my permanent record. Then Yang had added in a more ironic tone, “That being said, Knith Shade, for valor above and beyond the call of duty in adverse circumstances. And for the future you and your team have assured the fleet, it is with great honor that I award you another Heart Medalion for injury in the line of duty and the Leviathan Cross for valor.”

She went on. “You are to be advanced from your current rank as Private, to Brigade Captain. Congratulations and thank you for your service.” She made sure to have news orbs circling the conference room for that last part as she mugged for the cameras as she affixed the medals and Captain's Cluster to my armor.

That was mortifying and unneeded. I felt... well I felt like a failure. It was my job to protect everyone on the mission and I just about got each and every one of them killed. I had gotten Beta killed.

It wasn't until a week after that day when magi-tech technicians went over my experimental armor to determine why it couldn't interface with Mother, that I learned that I had been in error in that last assertion. I may or may not have had to hide a tear from the geeky engineers when they found that over a third of the instruction sets, and the bulk of the memory banks in the armor were occupied by a quantum encrypted memory engram from Mother.

I seriously felt joy when she moved it to the main data core and opened it. Beta, in her last moments, had shunted her final four hours of experiences into my scatter armor systems. It had sounded as if Mother cut back a sob when she said, “It's her... me. It's all here, even her, my, fear.”

She hadn't wanted to make a new Beta until that moment. And with a happy chirp, she had informed me that she'd get started right away on a new avatar.

Now here we all were, seeing not just Doc off, but Beta too. She looked like a kid in a candy shop because she wasn't connected to the data core, being in autonomous mode. She was actually bouncing on her toes on anticipation.

Imagine the shock to the Queens and President Yang when Mother had put in a vacation request. She was going to walkabout for a couple weeks with Doc, her Beta avatar disconnected from the endless tasks of monitoring all the ship's systems and people on board. Getting the chance to see what being an individual was like. It was pointed out that she held citizenship status now, and she hasn't had a vacation in five thousand years, so it was due.

It was hard for some to grasp the notion since Mother wouldn't really be on vacation since she was needed to run the Worldship so minorly inconvenient things like us all dying didn't occur. She was just allowing for a portion of herself to be shut out of her main systems to experience the world as we did for a while. As a person, an individual.

I thought it was brilliant, and I was interested to see how Beta's own personality would evolve over time being out of contact with her greater self.

I only wished Aurora could be here with us to see them off. She had been on my arm when we first arrived, but she got one of those Fairy shitting, mysterious calls and said as she stopped to reverse course, regret in her eyes as she said, “I'm sorry Knith. I really have to go. Please bid them safe travels for me?” Then she gave me a quick peck on the lips and dashed off with her guards.

I watched her go then asked, “Mother?”

“I don't feel comfortable about this, Knith,” she said.

“I just want to know she's safe.”

She huffed and sighed, “Fine. The parts I could decrypt before their magic blocked my systems from logging the call say something about a positive identification on the target.”

I sighed heavily. No matter how many times I tried bringing up the subject of these mysterious calls, and the disturbances on the world that seemed to be brushed under the rug at the highest levels, she somehow changed the subject. Well fine, she'd seduce me. So what if I didn't resist, I mean, you've seen my girl right? I was defenseless against that much sexy.

Grinning, I stepped to Beta and handed her a gift that cost me almost half a year's chit. I got it from a craftsman I know in the Beta-Ring. The same Elf who had carved my changing screen in my bedroom. An actual wooden, hand-carved walking stick. Wood was such a rare commodity on the world. The Fae controlled zealously, any wood that comes from the forests on the Alpha and Beta rings.

I said, “For your travels.” Then I waved off the start of her objections. “I know you never get tired, but it is symbolic of your journey.”

She had just blinked at it as she took it carefully, almost lovingly and said something that almost broke me because I had never ever given it any thought and I felt a little ashamed of it, “For... for me? Thank you so very much Knith! It is beautiful. I've... I've never owned anything before.”

Feeling as bad as the Fae for not thinking of that fact, I just hugged her. She made a happy contented sound. I assured her, “I'll do better.” She looked confused and I almost chuckled, since I assumed she knew what I was thinking, Mother is always in my head when I wear my helmet.

On cue, Mother said, “You just think too loud, Knith. She'll... I'll... oh this is so frustrating. We'll understand when Beta reconnects with the core in two weeks.”

I nodded and was about to say something when the Leviathan shook. I looked up through the translucent sky glass and down-ring over on the Gamma-Stack D-Ring. I saw an explosion ejecting debris from the bulkhead. Oh, space me now.

Moments later all hands were called to Gamma-D and I told the others, “I'm sorry, I've got to go! Doc, Beta, safe travels!”

Beta nodded as Doc waved, then Beta was grabbing my shoulders, and she was kissing me. “Thank you Knith. Don't endanger yourself while I'm gone.”

I was smiling in a little daze before the Worldship shook again, knocking me out of it. I said as I ran off, “I can't promise anything.”

She grumped, “Of course, you wouldn't be you if you didn't run toward danger.”

Graz was whistling. “Oh, man did she lay a lip lock on you. Again! You're lucky Princess Aurora is so open about sex.”

“Shut up.”

“I mean, that's the second time...”

“Shut up!” I mimed locking her lips with a key and throwing it away as I blurted, “Mother?”

She said, “Your Tac-Bike is arriving now.” She sounded a little put out. She caught the thought, and she said, “I know it's irrational, but when she kissed you.”

I chuckled to myself as I leapt onto my Tac-Bike a moment after bursting outside. “Jealous, of yourself? And hey, stop stealing kisses. I'm with Rory, remember?”

She pouted. “I know. And I know I'll have that experience when she reconnects. I'm just not used to being in two places at once. And Aurora and I have had a long talk about this subject and she is very understanding. She says if she ever... what was the old earth term? Kicked you to the curb? That I was welcome to you.”

I muttered to Graz, “I'm in the weirdest love triangle where I'm the only one who feels weird about it.”

The Greater Sprite started giggling as I snicked my visor down to protect us from the wind as I turned on the siren and lights and hit the emergency lane just above street level. “Hey, yer talkin' to a mated tri. It's all normal to me. And have you seen Beta's new form, I mean, I'd cross-pollinate with that if you catch my drift?”

I sighed, shaking my head. “I always get your drift, Graz. Now shut up, I've an emergency to get to, and I think Rory is involved.” She shut up, and I grudgingly had to agree with her. Not about pollinating anything that moved, but Mother certainly was pulling out all the stops to make her avatar attractive to me. And if I weren't already in a relationship...

“Aww, that's the nicest thing you've ever said to me.”

“Mother, get out of my head. I didn't say it, you're just eavesdropping on my...”

“Hold on, Knith. Incoming message.”

It started scrolling as I burped out into the trunk from the spoke we used to get down here, and I traversed over to one on Gamma-Stack. What in the hells was going on? Top priority message from Brigade HQ. All units and all emergency units are recalled. Skin jockeys are to standby to await the all-clear to repair the hull breach caused by accidental rupture of pressure vessels in the J-Bulkhead of Gamma-D. Enforcers are to keep civilians clear of the accident site until the all-clear is sounded.

Another cover-up? I growled out loud and Graz punched my nose, “Hey!”

She glared at me in a challenge, “Focus.”

Fine.

"I don't like what you're thinking, Knith," Mother said.

"Tough. Don't make me zip your lips too."

We reached the D-Ring and the Brigade already had formed a perimeter. I buzzed right past them as a commander was holding up a halting hand to me as I approached. I'm sure I'll hear about that soon. I normally hated flying my bike in the bulkhead corridors like some of the other Enforcers, but I was sick and tired of all the cloak and dagger bullshit going on that had my girl involved up to her neck in it.

I could hear smaller explosions as I poured on the speed in the evacuated corridors as I hugged the ceiling. I could feel the backwash of magic, some Fae, some not. Then I reached a blast door that was closed for no apparent reason as the controls showed there was an atmosphere on the other side.

I used my Enforcer emergency override code and the huge blast doors rose in their tracks. I blinked at the scene beyond. It looked like a war zone! The bulkhead walls had been torn apart, and there were bodies of dozens of preternatural strewn about the deck. My armor's overlays showed them all alive and breathing but severely injured.

And there, in the middle of the space, flanked by two raging Queens of the Fae, was Rory, her face bloodied and healing as she held a Minotaur off the ground by his neck with one hand. And she dropped him to the deck. He gasped and scrambled away from her. By the gods, she looked spectacular with her magic crackling about her. Like some sort of storm goddess bring down her wrath. I've never seen her looking so beautiful.

Mab looked around and said, “It is over.”

I whispered out, “Rory? What's happening here?”

She seemed to just then realize I was there and the magic and power bled away as she just blinked at me and asked, “Knith?”

I repeated my question as I strode cautiously up to the trio. And she looked suddenly shy as she said in a small voice, “Umm... hello.” She looked down at her waist and I realized a little hand was holding onto her from behind for dear life.

She said more clearly as she stood taller, her chin high as she said with an excited pleasure as she pulled an angelic-looking... Fae child? possibly six or seven years old, forward, and hugged her to her from behind, the little one hugged onto her arms as the little one looked at me with what felt like... awe? “Knith Shade, Enforcer of Beta-Stack, I'd like to introduce you to... your daughter.”

The world fell out from underneath me and my head started to spin as I just stared at the perfect little child... my... daughter?

The End

Novels by Erik Schubach

Books in the Worldship Files series...

Leviathan
Firewyrm
Cityships
Morrigan
Changeling (2021)

Books in the Techromancy Scrolls series...

Adept
Soras
Masquerade
Westlands
Avalon
New Cali
Colossus (2020)

Books in the Urban Fairytales series...

Red Hood: The Hunt
Snow: The White Crow
Ella: Cinders and Ash
Rose: Briar's Thorn
Let Down Your Hair
Hair of Gold: Just Right
The Hood of Locksley
Beauty In the Beast
No Place Like Home
Shadow Of The Hook
Armageddon

Books in the New Sentinels series...

Djinn: Cursed
Raven Maid: Out of the Darkness
Fate: No Strings Attached
Open Seas: Just Add Water
Ghost-ish: Lazarus
Anubis: Death's Mistress
Sentinels: Reckoning (2020)

Books in the Drakon series...

Awakening
Dragonfall

Books in the Valkyrie Chronicles series...
Return of the Asgard
Bloodlines
Folkvangr
Seventy Two Hours
Titans

Books in the Tales From Olympus series...
Gods Reunited
Alfheim
Odyssey

Books in the Bridge series...
Trolls
Traitor
Unbroken
Krynn

Books in the Fracture series...
Divergence

Novellas by Erik Schubach

The Hollow

Novellas in the Paranormals series...
Fleas
This Sucks
Jinx (2020)

Novellas in the Fixit Adventures...
Fixit
Glitch
Vashon
Descent
Sedition

Novellas in the Emily Monroe Is Not The Chosen One series...
Night Shift
Unchosen
Rechosen (2020)

Short Stories by Erik Schubach

(These short stories span many different genres)

A Little Favor
Lost in the Woods
MUB
Mirror Mirror On The Wall
Oops!
Rift Jumpers: Faster Than Light
Scythe
Snack Run
Something Pretty

Romance Novels by Erik Schubach

Books in the Music of the Soul universe...

(All books are standalone and can be read in any order)

Music of the Soul
A Deafening Whisper
Dating Game
Karaoke Queen
Silent Bob
Five Feet or Less
Broken Song
Syncopated Rhythm
Progeny
Girl Next Door
Lightning Strikes Twice
June
Dead Shot

Music of the Soul Shorts...

(All short stories are standalone and can be read in any order)

Misadventures of Victoria Davenport: Operation Matchmaker
Wallflower
Accidental Date
Holiday Morsels
What Happened In Vegas?

Books in the London Harmony series...

(All books are standalone and can be read in any order)

Water Gypsy
Feel the Beat
Roctoberfest
Small Fry
Doghouse
Minuette
Squid Hugs
The Pike
Flotilla

Books in the Pike series...

(All books are standalone and can be read in any order)

Ships In The Night
Right To Remain Silent
Evermore
New Beginnings

Books in the Flotilla series...

(All books are standalone and can be read in any order)

Making Waves
Keeping Time
The Temp
Paying the Toll

Books in the Unleashed series...

Case of the Collie Flour
Case of the Hot Dog
Case of the Gold Retriever
Case of the Great Danish
Case of the Yorkshire Pudding
Case of the Poodle Doodle
Case of the Hound About Town
Case of the Shepherd's Pie
Case of the Bull Doggish
Case of the Dalmatian Salvation